PSYCH

PATRICIA ELEBY

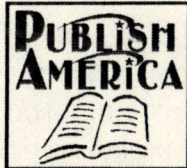

PublishAmerica

PublishAmerica
Baltimore

First printing

ISBN: 1-4137-2089-7
PUBLISHED BY PUBLISHAMERICA, LLLP
www.publishamerica.com
Baltimore

Printed in the United States of America

This book is dedicated to my, cousin, Tony Jones.
I miss you.

Acknowledgements

First, I would like to give honor to My Lord and Savior Jesus Christ for all his many blessings. To my children Keysha Sharie, Felicia Nadine, and my nieces, Chrisandra Smith, Jamella Nicole Speech and my nephew, John H. Long IV for giving me the inspiration to write this book. To my loving husband, Ben, I love you and thank you for putting up with my craziness. Thank you to my mother, Jane O. Long and father, John H. Long Sr. for giving me love and encouragement whenever I needed it. My brother, John, you're my buddy and I will always have your back. To my Aunt Josephine Lindsay, and Mr. Lewis R. Coles, thank you for being there through the trying times of my life, and for all of your words of encouragement. To my cousin, Alice, thanks for the memories, we had a ball, didn't we? To all my aunts, uncles, and cousins in Philly and abroad, I love you all. To my best friends in the world, Vanessa Reid and Lavonne Speech-Long, thank you for your guidance and critique-ness, and for dealing with my insanity. To everyone at Lutheran Children and Family Service, I've never met such lovely people in my life! Last, but not least, a special thank you to Mr. Brian J. Loebig and Mrs. Yvette Bradford, thank you for teaching me all of the different computer programs and for caring.

PROLOGUE
THE DEATH

On a frigid, winter evening in December the sky was black and the moon danced among the stars. The air was crisp and cold as the wind dashed around corners to hide, awaiting its next victim to gust upon. The stars shining through the blanket of darkness cast their luminous glow of light sparsely, and the night had an eerie feeling.

The automobiles moved through the streets of Philadelphia in rapid succession, as if everyone had somewhere to go. All those people going nowhere fast, as the other cars across the street moved slowly as if to a funeral procession. The sounds of the beeping vehicles and engines passing by made Jade wish she was driving instead of strolling in the cold night air.

It was 7 o'clock on Thursday evening when Jade Wilson was walking home from her night-school dance class. She had practiced all week for her recital, which was scheduled to take place the next night. She was a little afraid and wondered if she would do a good job, but she knew deep down in her heart that she would do more than exceptional. After all, Jade had her mother's spirit and her father's moves; dancing had been her family's talent for over five generations.

Her grandmother danced with the Rockettes for over 20 years, even after she met her grandfather. They became a dance team and often auditioned for musicals when her grandfather had time between working as a bellhop to help support his growing family. Her grandmother did the best she could raising a daughter and a son. Her biggest fear was wondering if she would ever make it to Broadway someday, but she worried constantly about her children.

She often thought about leaving the Rockettes to become a full-time mother and a few times she did, but by some means she always went back to her first love, dancing.

As Jade came to an intersection that wasn't too far from her home she paused for a moment to take in her neighborhood. Most of the buildings were built back in the 60's but had a colonial feel. Some occupants had modified the outside of their homes with siding, and there were patios in front of some, but all of the homes had well manicured lawns out front. They all had two steps that followed to the front doors, and most of them had two large shrubberies in the yard and magnificent picture or bay windows. Throughout the holidays those same windows would come alive with all the Christmas trimmings. It seemed that each of her neighbors put in long hours to make their windows and properties outshine the rest.

During the summer months everyone would gather on those same steps to talk about what was going on in the neighborhood or what was going on in their lives. Most of the teenagers were middle-class, but some were poor and no one seemed to care. They all enjoyed each other's company. Hanging out on the front stoop or at the mall took away most of the heartaches that came with growing up. Jade thought back on the time when she and Nadine stayed out one summer night talking about boyfriends, school, and people on the block until the wee hours of the morning.

She passed Sharie's house. Nadine, her best friend, lived two blocks down and around the corner. She contemplated about going to her house; however, there was a feeling of precaution riveted through her body like a lightning bolt. The sensation increased as the wind blew through her long, black hair as she continued down to her house. Shoulders up, along with her collar to block out the cold air around her neck, she kept her hands in her pockets. Jade was angry with herself for leaving her hat and gloves home. At home she felt she would be safe. She sensed someone was watching her every move, but when she turned around to look no one was there. Abruptly, Jade felt an urge to run to her house, yet as soon as she thought it, she caught a glimpse of someone retreating into the shadows, moving in

6

and out of the bushes from across the street. She knew she saw something, but couldn't quite make out what or whom it was. As she headed for her steps, beads of sweat appeared on her forehead; the sweat made her skin feel sticky and clammy.

She continued to run to her house but saw the same figure again. This time closer, she could see that it was tall with long-limbed arms. It was wearing a black leather coat that flowed like a cape in the wind. Its hat was pre-twenty first century and its suit was ebony black with gold trim around the collar and gold buttons down the front of the jacket. He wore black gloves, but still she couldn't make out his face. She could feel its aura, and she knew she was in trouble.

Jade tried to make a quick dash for her front door, but before she could reach the first step she saw a bizarre person staring her right in the eye. Its face was covered with a Halloween mask that took on the figure of a fearful clown. Its long black hair hung shoulder length. As she stood in horror, it grabbed her by her neck and lifted her several inches from the ground. The over worn, holey, ripped up, rough gloves constricted her air.

She perceived what looked like a knife come from behind it ripping through the side of her neck hitting her jugular vein. She tried to fight back and remove its mask to unveil her attacker, but her body was suspended in mid air. Before it lifted her in the air, she managed to slash at its coat with her fingernails but she could not reach its face. She could feel the blood run slowly down her neck and the pain of the knife still embedded and covered with her blood.

Her demented killer unmercifully removed the knife from his slowly dying victim. It dropped her lifeless body and mistakenly dropped the weapon on the ground. Only later would he discover the knife was missing.

Jade's screams for help went unnoticed and useless, all she could remember was the face of a clown as her limp, cold body gave way to the darkness. Jade's life slowly and painfully left her. The strangest thing that she last remembered was the pinch of a needle in her arm. All she could see was darkness.

CHAPTER 1
IT HAPPENS

Eighteen year old Nadine sat by the window in her room staring into the dark night holding her cat, Twiggy, wondering what she would wear to the school dance on Friday night. She had already gone through her closet several times, but couldn't find anything to her liking. She thought about asking her parents for the money for a new dress, being that she wouldn't get paid from her job down at the boutique until the week after the dance. *Mom would have it*, she thought, but then again she knew how her mom felt about money. *A penny saved is a penny earned*, her mother would say. She thought about asking Dad, *Yeah!* That sounded like a plan; Dad would surely come through. *I'm sure he won't refuse me, being that he just got paid last night.*

Nadine's father worked as a forklift driver at the Acme Corrugated Box Company for over 20 years. He was close to his retirement and couldn't wait to spend the rest of his days lounging about the house or on the sandy beaches of Atlantic City in the summer. Nadine would have to wait until her dad was at the breakfast table reading his morning paper. That was the time he was most vulnerable to suggestion, but she decided against it and thought about asking that very instant.

She got up from the window and lay horizontally on her bed on her back with her stuffed animals and Twiggy, and stared at the ceiling. Nadine appeared to be older than her age. She was cute and sexy, her boyfriend often told her. Her skin was chocolate brown and her eyes were slanted as if she were of Chinese decent. She was slender and thought she looked good, especially in her jeans. *I'm just so sexy!*

She lay there on her bed still gazing at the ceiling. Her room was painted lavender with shelves full of stuffed animals around the room that she collected over the years. To the left of the small room were her awards. A vanity sat under those accomplishments. On the vanity were the pictures of her boyfriend, Mark, that they took on a date to the local carnival. Posters of her favorite WWE wrestlers hung on the wall to the right. Her room was *her* domain and she kept it spotless.

As she laid with her stuffed animals, still pondering about the dance, Nadine thought for sure her friends, Sharie and Nicole, would be there. However, she wasn't too sure about Chris. Chris was her friend even though she could be a know-it-all pain in the butt. Nadine appreciated Chris for her generosity and her broad-mindedness. Sometimes she would have to pull her away from a mirror and saved her numerous times from flirting with the boys, but that was a thing they both loved to do. Chris always busied herself with her studies. She seldom had time to hang out with her friends. Whenever they got together, nine times out of ten, she and Nadine had a blast. But still Nadine hoped.

Putting the cat down on the floor, she moved from her bed and inspected her closet again. She picked out a dress that she thought would be ok to wear for her big night. It was purple with a low v cut in the front. Her mother bought her that 3 years ago. Nadine held the dress up and examined herself in front of her floor length mirror. She noticed that she had a grown a few inches since she last wore it. Nadine knew for sure the dress would be too short. Her hips had become more round as she matured into womanhood. She was a pretty girl and the guys liked her a lot. She often thought she was too tall, but the guys didn't seem to mind. Her boyfriend, Mark, often told her how beautiful she was even though she stood an inch taller than he was. Although she wasn't happy about her physical appearance, Nadine was happy.

She was smart, intelligent and pretty. Her face oval shaped, eyes brown like the color of walnuts and her lips were full. She took pleasure every time she put on lipstick. Her mother thought she looked her best in pink, but she didn't. She did exceptionally well in school; enough to earn her a 4-year scholarship to UCLA.

Nadine hung her dress back and removed her robe that hung on the inside of the closet door. She threw it on over top of her flowered red, flannel pj's and headed downstairs, where her mom and dad sat watching *The Practice.*

The living room was positioned to the left of the stairs. Standing at the bottom step, anyone could see the glass table with the black lamp. The living room was medium sized, family photos hung against the beige walls along with a few African artifacts and paintings of lions and cheetahs in the Savannah bush. In the window was a large, unusual vase that held painted gold and black, artificial flowers behind the bay window, where gold painted, vertical blinds hung from the top of the window down to the floor. The curtains matched the walls of the living room and hung to the floor; neatly tied to the sides. In front of the window was the off-beige love seat. Her father sat on the matching couch lengthwise with his feet in the chair, reading the evening paper. She peeked in on them and decided to join them. Nadine sat down in the love seat next to her mom.

Louise Johnson was a straight forward type of woman who tried to raise her daughter with love and respect for all things. She was deeply religious and attended church regularly. She was even the president of the Sunday school program. Louise was a heavy set woman with short black hair, and big brown eyes that seemed to dance when she smiled. Her skin was like smooth creamy caramel, but age was starting to catch up with her. She just turned 40 and you could tell from the bags that started to form under her eyes. She worked as an Administrative Assistant for Lutheran Children and Family Service.

Nadine's father, Hoover, was a dark skinned man, like the hue of an Oreo cookie. He was short with thinning hair that he kept low and to his forehead. His eyes were black as coal and his presence filled the air whenever he walked into a room. He was the head of the household and he never let his wife or daughter forget it. He was a force to be reckoned with, but he had a heart of gold and would go out of his way for anyone. He too attended church and was chairman of the deacon board.

Her mother turned away from the television to face her only child, "How was school today, honey?" she asked reverently.

"Mmm, so, so," Nadine replied nonchalantly. She turned her head sideways and let out a sigh with a look of boredom on her face. "I got a B plus on my science report."

"Really? That's great honey," her mother said. "Before you know it you'll be graduating and you'll be in UCLA." Her mother's face lit up with a smile, she hugged her and kissed her forehead.

Her father lowered the paper to show her his eyes of contentment then continued reading.

"I talked to my counselor, Mr. Mathews, today. He thinks I have a good chance of getting into some local colleges as well, but I hope that Chris won't be too far from me, or either I hope she'll go to the same college as me."

"Don't bank on it, Nadine. Being that she made the honor roll so many times, I know colleges will be banging down her door."

"Yeah, you're right, Mom, but I can still hope," said Nadine with a kooky smile on her face.

Her mother returned the smile and turned back to the television. Nadine wanted to say something else, but her mother stopped her with a raised hand before she could make a sound. A special report broke in from the Channel 6-News room. A handsome anchorman, Jim Gardner, was dressed in a gray suit and matching tie where his miniature microphone was attached. His hair was dark brown with a distinguished touch of white around the side burns and top of his face. He looked to be younger than his early fifties. He sat with his face in a serious form.

"This just in to Action News. A murder has just occurred in the West Oak Lane section of the city for further information we go to Vernon Odom, who's live at the scene. Vernon?"

The television screen switched to a tall African American man in his late 40's dressed in a black leather coat. His brown suit peeked through along with his beige tie and white shirt. He held the microphone in his hand that had the Channel 6 logo on the face. He stood across the street in front of the home of Jade Wilson. In the background, yellow crime scene tape was placed around the two bushes that led to the front of the house extending around the old oak tree. To the left was a coroner's vehicle that read Benjamin Bannaker Memorial Hospital on the side door. To the immediate right were police cars and an ambulance, public officials, investigators and forensic scientists. They were walking and searching around the crime scene wearing plastic gloves and carrying plastic bags. One official marked the area where Jade's body was found with white chalk.

The door to Jade Wilson's home was open; everyone watching at home could see Mr. and Mrs. Wilson embracing each other while sitting on the couch talking to a police officer. Standing to the right of the house was Sharie, and her mother and a few neighbors. Sharie held her mother and cried on her shoulders.

"Earlier tonight," Vernon continued, "18-year-old Jade Wilson was coming home from her dance class when she was brutally attacked by an unknown assailant. Information is sketchy at this time, but police do have the murder weapon. I have here with me, the homicide detective, in charge of this case, Bradley Rayford."

Rayford came into view wearing a black full-length, double collar leather coat that zipped in the front and snapped at the top. Underneath he wore a yellow turtleneck. He looked rather mysterious in his matching black full grain leather hat and gloves. His jacket concealed his black cotton pants.

Vernon turned to face Rayford and asked, "Detective tell us what happened?"

"Well," Rayford began, "we believe the assailant approached Miss Wilson from the rear. Bloody foot prints were discovered in the area approximately ten feet away from were Miss Wilson's body was found. This was a horrible act of violence. There's no doubt in my mind about that. We're gathering all the evidence and we've confiscated the murder weapon. We've had that taken to forensics to be analyzed and hopefully we'll have more answers in a few days."

"Were there any witnesses?"

"Only one and we are still questioning that person at the moment."

"Thank you, Detective, for your time I know you must get back to your work," Vernon said.

Rayford slowly stepped out of the camera's view. The camera panned back to Vernon. He turned back to face the cameras again.

"Neighbors of Miss Wilson say that she was a well loved person and an exceptionally intelligent young women who would have graduated from Rosa Parks High School this year."

The camera switched to two men putting Jade's body into the coroner's vehicle covered in a body bag on a Gurney. Nadine's parents sat and watched in horror. Before Louise could grab a hold of her daughter, Nadine made a mad dash out the door as her parents fell in pursuit. Nadine ran up the street. When she got to the second block she cut through a neighbor's alley way in the middle of the block. In an instant she could see Vernon and the bright lights. The coroner's car was about to pull off as she came to the clearing.

Nadine ran after the car crying hysterically and screaming; she fell to the ground screaming her best friend's name. Sharie left her mother's side and ran after Nadine and held her. She continued to scream. At that moment Nadine's parents caught up to her and held their daughter and Sharie in the middle of the street. Nadine's friends, Nicole and Chris, came running down the street to their friends' aid. They too saw the special report and huddled around Nadine, Sharie and her parents crying and wishing for answers.

~ ~ ~ ~

Friday morning, 18-year-old Sharie Thompson awoke to the smell of bacon and eggs cooking downstairs. She didn't get much sleep from the previous night, but she sheepishly wiped her eyes and at a snail's pace headed off to the bathroom. She took a shower, brushed her teeth, and went back to her room. She didn't feel up to going to school today either, but she knew Jade wouldn't want her to stay home and mope. She walked over to her closet and opened it. Sharie stood there for a moment examining herself in front of her mirror that hung on the back door. Her face was oval, and her skin was caramel colored and smooth like a baby's bottom. Her black hair flowed down her shoulders when she left it out, but she always kept it in a ponytail. She stood about 5'6" and stocky.

Her mother and grandmother often tried to talk to her about dropping a few pounds, but she thought she looked just fine. She carefully picked out her clothes for that day. She decided on her FUBU jeans, white t-shirt, blue socks and white Nike Air Force Ones sneakers. She thought about putting on her new Timberland's, but she didn't feel up to breaking them in yet. She got dressed then made her bed and grabbed her backpack and hurried off downstairs where she found her mother sitting in the kitchen drinking coffee and reading the morning paper.

Her mother quickly folded it because she didn't want her daughter to see it. Jade's murder had made the front page of the *Daily News*. Mrs. Thompson was still in her red nightgown with her burgundy robe covering her; it tied around her small waist. Her hair was tightly put in a bun. She had to leave for work by eight. Her boss, Mr. Hernandez, at Light House Adoption Agency would not tolerate her being late.

Her mother was an Executive Secretary for 8 years with the agency and she loved knowing that her work helped so many less fortunate children find safe and loving homes. She turned sideways in her chair and turned to face her daughter as she entered the room. Sharie looked at her, puzzled as to why her mother folded the paper so fast, and questioned her.

"Mom, why are you acting so strange this morning?"

"Oh, good morning dear. Did you sleep okay?" her mother said with a non-shalant secretive face.

"No, not really. Mom, you're avoiding my question. Why did you fold the paper so fast? Is it because Jade's murder is on the front cover by any chance?" Her mother let out a sigh.

"Yes dear, and I didn't want to upset you. Are you going to be okay today at school?"

"Yeah, I think so. I just kept thinking all last night about who would do this and why?" Tears started to appear again.

"I understand if you don't want to go to school today, honey."

"No, Mom. Jade would want me to go. I know that."

"Are you still going to the dance tonight?" her mother inquired.

"I guess so. The dance starts at 7 p.m. So, when I get home I'll probably change over at Chris' house so that we can leave together. I'm not sure if Nadine will go or not. From what her mom told me on the phone last night, their doctor had to give her a sedative."

"Baby, I don't know about this. They haven't caught this guy yet. It was on the news again this morning that they have no clue as to who did it. He's still out there Sharie, and I don't want to risk you getting hurt or worse getting killed!" she said in a firm tone.

"Mom, I'm a big girl now and I can take care of myself, so don't worry."

"I don't like this and my gut feeling is telling me not to let you go."

"Mom, I'll be with Nadine and her date, as well as, Nicole and Chris and their dates, plus they'll be chaperones at the dance. I'll be fine," she said reassuring her.

"Alright, but I want you to call me on your way over to Chris' house and then stop by the house on your way out so that I can take a look at that dress. Be careful when you girls leave," her mother said.

"I will, Mom," she said as she grabbed a plate from the kitchen cabinet. "I'm going to miss her; she was like a sister to me," Sharie said wiping her eyes. "Does anybody know when her funeral will be?" she inquired. Grabbing her food from stove, she then took a seat next to her mother and began picking at her food.

"Next Tuesday at 9 a.m. Mr. Snow told me. I know her parents must be going through hell right now, and the worse thing about it is nobody knows anything. You have to keep your kids closer to you these days".

"Mom, I told you I'd be ok," Sharie said.

"Honey, I'm a mother and I can't help but worry about you. And if I haven't told you lately, I
love you," her mother said. She got up from the table and hugged her.

"I know, Mom. I love you too," she assured her mother as she finished her food and gave her mother a big hug, then grabbed her jacket from behind her chair.

"Sharie, please come back here about six so I can see you off, ok?"

"I will."

"You promise?"

"I promise Mom."

"Be careful when you girls leave," her mother said. "Have a good day at school and I'll see you after you get dressed."

"Okay. Bye Mom."

"Bye, honey." She closed the kitchen door and was gone.

Don't worry, huh? I'll be on pins and needles 'til you get back here,' her mother thought.

~ ~ ~ ~

As Nadine made her way out to her black 1995 Ford Taurus, she looked down the street and noticed the police tape that encircled the area where the horrible murder took place. She couldn't help but walk down and get a better look at it. As she got within inches of the scene, she noticed the bloodstains on the bottom step and the white chalk that outlined where her friend's body laid and where the murder weapon was found. She didn't want to remember what took place here. She couldn't fathom why someone would do this.

She turned and made a B-line back to her car when, she saw Jade's mother peek out of her front window with tears in her eyes. Nadine stared at her for a moment. *My heart goes out to her,* she thought, *and I'll never forget her*, as the tears came again. She pulled her car keys out, unlocked the door and started the engine and sped off to school.

~ ~ ~ ~

Chris pulled up in the teachers' parking lot in her red 1998 Plymouth Duster. He noticed Sharie and how tall and beautiful she was. Her mother told her a few times that she looked like a string bean because of her weight, but then in her next breath she would tell her that she was getting fat. Still, in all, she was cute. Her big brown eyes sometimes over powered her beautiful smile. Her eyes always attracted the opposite sex. Her skin was the color of a Hershey bar, and she liked the way her skin seemed to glow in the sunlight. She kept her long black hair natural and braided. She didn't trust perms and other chemicals in her hair. Sometimes she would wear her hair out, and when she did she looked like an African Queen. She was dressed casually today in her blue jeans and blue cotton Rockaware pull-over shirt.

Nadine, of course, was dressed too dramatic as usual. She wore a black buttoned silk shirt with rhinestones covering the shoulder. Her shirt was unbuttoned too low and her black skirt came to her ankles.

Nicole, who had been short and chunky all of her life, wore a white blouse with a red and white checkered pleated skirt. She was cute and full of spunk, but she was naïve. Her complexion was fair, giving her round face a porcelain doll appearance. Her brown eyes seemed to dance whenever she would smile.

They all arrived together at the school. Sharie quickly shut off the engine, took her keys out, grabbed her book bag, got out and locked the door so she could catch up with her fellowcomrades.

"Hey guys."

"Hey," they all said in unison.

Sharie got in stride with the rest of her friends as they all walked together. No one spoke. Sharie finally broke the silence.

"Come on, guys. I know we all feel bad about what happened, but Jade wouldn't want us all sad like this. She would want us to be happy and continue on with our lives."

"We all know that, Sharie, but it still doesn't ease the pain," Nadine said.

"Well, I don't know about you guys, but I'm going to find out who did this. I will not let her death go in vain!" Nadine said.

"And how do you purpose to do that?" asked Sharie.

"I'm going to do my own detective work. I know the officer that was there last night and he comes in the boutique a lot. He's the coach of the basketball team and I'll probably catch him when I go into work tonight," said Nadine.

"What makes you think that he'll tell you anything?" asked Chris.

"I don't know. But he's a good friend of my boss, Mrs. Washington. I can easily eves drop on their conversations when he comes in the store. I don't know if I can speak for everybody else, but I'm going to find out who did this."

"Yeah, I'm in too," said Sharie and Chris. They all turned to look at Nicole.

"What can I do?" she asked.

"Just be our eyes and ears that all," said Sharie.

"I won't promise you guys it will be all roses. We have to be careful. This could be dangerous and we can't tell our parents what we're doing," Nadine suggested.

They all stopped and held hands as they swore and made a pack between all of them. Sharie turned to Chris.

"Chris, did you get the notes from history class yesterday? Mr. Brinkley erased the board before I could get it all down. He's such an ass clown."

"Isn't that the truth! But anyway, yeah. I got the notes for you. I'll give it to you when we get in school."

"All right cool," said Sharie.

~ ~ ~ ~

They all continued walking and talked about how they would go about their plan. They got to the front steps of Rosa Parks High and started filing in with the rest of the teenagers.

"Chris, I need those notes before we go in because I got to go to my locker before I go to history. I got ass clown first period," Sharie requested. Chris pulled out her history notebook on the steps and gave it to her.

"Don't loose my notes. I need them for next weeks test," she said.

"I won't."

"You'll get them back by the end of the day, I promise."

~ ~ ~ ~

Sharie had caught up with Chris at lunchtime and told her that she would stop by her house to change for the dance.

"You're still going?" asked Chris.

"Yes."

"Okay, well, I'll meet you outside of the center, but I have to tell you I thought about not going."

"Why?"

"Why?" she repeated sarcastically. "What the hell do you think? Because of what happened to Jade! Fool! And because I don't have a date."

"I know!" she said with a sad face. "But I thought you said James asked you to go?"

"He did and I said I would, but then Mr. Jamison told us we had a test coming up this Friday."

"I wasn't about to go either with all that's happened, but I think we should. Jade would have wanted it that way, don't you think?"

"Yeah, she would have. I'm sure going to miss her and I know she would have loved to be at the dance with us. Dancing was her favorite thing," Chris said in deep thought.

"Yeah, well, I told my mom that I would come over your house to change and she said she wanted to see me in my dress before I go."

"Okay. I'll see you at my house around 5."

"See ya," said Chris.

"See ya later," Sharie replied in return.

CHAPTER 2
THE INVESTIGATION

It was a busy day down at the 103rd precinct besides people being booked and finger printed for whatever crimes they committed. Captain Jennings' phone was practically ringing off the hook with fearful civilians wanting to know if they had any leads on the murder of Jade Wilson. He had to take his phone off the hook momentarily letting the calls patch through the station's operator. He was getting tired of trying to tell people that he could not give out that sort of information. He could only reassure them that they were on top of things and would soon have the case solved. His office was full of clutter. Papers everywhere on his desk, on his file cabinets and some were stacked on the floor behind him. To the right sat pictures of his wife and two kids.

The room was aligned with blinds that he kept open so he could see what was going on in the precinct. His office was on the 20th floor giving him a good view of the city skyline. Often he would be deep in thought while staring down at the pedestrians passing by. His filing cabinet, which he never kept in order, was off to the left of the room. He had awards and plaques that were given to him by the mayor and other prominent people for his outstanding work in the community. They hung on the wall to the right. He was proud of his accomplishments and all the officers under him respected and looked up to him.

Jennings was an older man. His face started to show his age from the wrinkles that started to form around his face. His skin was pale and his face turned cherry red whenever he would get angry. His stature was short and he considered himself chubby. His hair was gray and his mustache took on the same color.

He wore a burgundy dress shirt with a gray and burgundy striped tie. His pants were navy with quarter top pockets. His gut hung over the top of his pants. He had been meaning to drop a few pounds, but could never find the time for the exercise. His wife of 20 years, Doreen, tried everything in the book to put him on a strict diet. But each time he would throw away the lunches she would make for him and head to the nearest McDonald's.

He sat back with his feet on his desk reviewing the case that just came into his office. He was bewildered and he hated when he couldn't get a fix on things. He went over and over in his mind about the crime scene trying to think of a motive. He thought about any suspects that may have wanted to harm Jade as he stared at the fingerprints. He threw the papers on his desk got up and called out into the outer office for Detective Bradley Rayford.

"Rayford!"

"Yes, Sir!" came the stern reply.

"My office. NOW!"

"Yes, Sir" replied again.

~ ~ ~ ~

Bradley Rayford was an average sized man with long jet-black hair that he kept in a ponytail that accented his bright blue eyes. He sort of reminded everyone of the boy next-door, clean cut and muscular. He was handsome and very much in shape. He worked out in the gym two to three times a week and watched his diet. He was taller than his captain and often joked with his peers about how short the captain was.

Rayford was proficient in his work and the captain liked that about his officers. He hoped one day to get promoted to district attorney, but he felt he couldn't handle that position yet. *Two kids in college, a wife and a home? When would he find the time to spend with his wife?* he often thought. He was a family man and he loved his wife dearly; she always worried about him. She only agreed to let him join the academy because she knew once he had his mind set on something there was no reasoning with him. He was stubborn, but he had a flair for solving cases. Rayford entered the captains' office.

"Sit down, Bradley." he said calmly. "Bradley, I'm having trouble with this case you gave me. Did any of the other officers find any other evidence as to what happened to this young lady?"

"Well, Sir..." Rayford started, but was cut off by Jennings, who he now saw was getting upset.

"Don't 'well sir' me, Bradley! Damn it! Give it to me straight!" demanded the captain.

"Okay, we've covered every inch of the crime scene and all we could find was the murder weapon. Whoever this person is didn't do very well covering his or her tracks," stated Rayford.

"Listen, I want you to go back out to that house, question the parents, look over the scene again. Question the neighbors again. Maybe they remember something that they couldn't when you first questioned them."

"Did you get any prints off of the knife that you found? What became of the footprints sighted at the crime scene?"

"I'm waiting for the results from forensics as we speak, Sir. I'm planning on going to her school to question all of her friends."

"Good, while you're waiting for the test to come back, go out to the crime scene and don't come back here until you can come up with some answers. Do you hear me? I want names! I don't care what you have to do to get them. I want them pronto and I'm not kidding, Bradley. I want this crazy bastard! Do I make myself clear? My ass is on the line here, Detective! I've got the mayor and the district attorney breathing down my back! Oh, and by the way, on your way back stop by the coroner's office and see if the results are in."

"Will do, Sir." Rayford rose from his seat and turned to head out the door. He didn't want to hear anymore of the captain's *shit.*

~ ~ ~ ~

Later on that afternoon Bradley Rayford made a left turn at the intersection of Judson and Valley Road in his used 1999 blue Buick Lasable. He kept it in good condition, had it inspected and it just had a tune up. He pulled up in front of Jade's house around 4:30 pm. He got out of the car and walked around the crime scene tape that was still there. He was careful where he walked not wanting to disturb anything that could still be left behind. He bent down to get a good look over the area. *Nothing*, he thought to himself. He got up and walked over to the grass area and went over it again with a fine toothed-comb. His peripheral vision caught something between the grass and the walkway. It was a button; a gold button that looked like it came from someone's shirt or pants. He bent down pulling out his tweezers and a plastic bag and put the button inside. *I can't believe those ass hole officers disregarded this or either they're blind as hell!* he thought.

Rayford got up and headed for the door to Jade's house. He knocked and rang the doorbell. After waiting a few minutes he heard a female voice come from behind the door.

"Who is it?" the woman said.

"It's Detective Rayford from the 103rd precinct ma'am. Is Mr. or Mrs. Wilson home? I really need to speak with them." The door came open half way. A woman in her early 40's answered the door.

"May I see some I.D, please?" she asked cautiously.

"Ma'am I was just here the other night," Rayford said.

"I know, but you can't be too careful these days."

He looked at her strangely as she stared at him waiting patiently to see the detective's badge. He looked at her for a minute and then realized she was waiting for him to produce what she asked for.

"Oh sorry, here." He flashed it at her. "May I come in?" She opened the screen door and let him inside. He came into the vestibule that led into the living room. He noticed how well Mrs. Wilson kept her home. *"Very tidy, very nice,"* he said to himself. The living room had a relaxed feel to it. Family pictures sat on the mantle; portraits of Jade when she was younger. Some pictures of the whole family together.

The living room was painted sky blue with a white sectional couch that took up the majority of the room. The coffee table that sat in front of the huge couch was square with a glass tabletop and black lacquer legs; the entire table was trimmed with gold. A grandfather clock stood adjacent to the entertainment center that held the 32" screen TV. The room had an archway that led to the dinning room and further back you could see part of the kitchen. All of the furniture looked brand new including the dinning room set.

The dinning room was beige with pictures neatly hung on the walls. The china closet was made out of white lacquer with glass doors where she displayed her fine china that was black. Several crystal statues were strategically place accenting the cabinet that shined and glittered for optimal effect. The table and chairs matched the china closet.

Mrs. Wilson offered Bradley a seat on the sectional. She sat next to him.

"You have a very nice home here, Ma'am," said Bradley.

"Thank you" she said. "My husband is not at home at the moment. He felt he should go in to the office to try to keep his mind off of all this."

"I understand, ma'am."

"Can I get you some coffee or something?" she asked.

"No, ma'am, I'm fine."

"Well, then what can I help you with today? I told you everything I know already."

"I know, ma'am, but is there anything else you could think of that you may have forgotten?"

"I don't see what else there is to tell, Detective," she sighed. "Besides, if I knew who did this to my child you would be questioning me in front of my lawyer behind bars! But I really haven't had time to think about anything else. I've been busy trying to make funeral arrangement and so forth. I haven't slept a wink since all this happened."

"I know, ma'am, and I understand." Rayford apologized, "But there has to be something. Did Jade have any enemies? Any boyfriends or friends that may have had a grudge or something against her?"

"No. Jade was a sweet girl and everybody loved her. I never knew all of her friends, but the ones that I did know, never had any problems with her. Her boyfriend, Skyler, is a nice boy. We met him a few times," Mrs. Wilson explained. She tried to continue, but the emptiness of her daughter's absences came back and she had to pardon herself. "I'm sorry, Detective. This is too painful." She reached for a tissue on the coffee table.

"I know, ma'am, but in order for us to get this creep off the streets we have to find him or her. We need to gather up as much information as we can." He reached for her hand and held it gently to console her. Rayford could see that she had not slept and she looked tired and weak, but he knew he had to continue. He thought he would ask one more question and then leave.

"Mrs. Wilson, you mentioned that Jade had a boyfriend named Skyler?"

"Yes, he lives a few blocks away, but Jade told me the other day that he was going away for few days and wouldn't be home until tomorrow." She suddenly remembered. "Oh, God. He has no idea!" she started to cry again.

Rayford felt sorry for the woman. But he had to continue to question her.

"What's his address, ma'am?"

She told him the address. Bradley pulled out his pad and wrote down it down then he flipped the page and wrote down his office and cell phone number and handed it to her.

"Ma'am, here's my number if you remember anything or need to talk. You can reach me at these numbers."

"Thank you," she said and she took the number.

He stood up and headed for the door.

"I appreciate your time, Ma'am," he said as she stood and walked to the front door and opened it for him to let him out.

"If my husband or I remember anything we'll give you a call. I want this person brought to justice and prosecuted to the full extent!" she said with tears in her eyes.

"We'll get 'em, ma'am, don't worry," he said.

"Thank you," she said.

Rockford headed in the opposite direction of his car towards Skyler's house.

~ ~ ~ ~

Chris met up with Sharie outside of the community center on time. She left her job at Benjamin Bannaker Memorial Hospital. She worked part time as a nurse assistant. She liked her job even thought that was not the field she wanted to go into after graduation. She wanted to be a singer, but her parents wouldn't have it. So, she chose nursing instead. She already looked over some brochures for what nursing school she might be interested in attending, but she wasn't fond of any of her choices.

"Sharie, did you get the dress?"

"Yeah, I stopped by Nadine's job on my break and picked out something. It's in the back of my car," she stated.

"Man, I'll be glad when I get my car out of the shop. I'm tired of the busses and walking."

"I know what you mean," said Sharie.

They walked over across the street where Sharie's car was parked. Sharie popped open the trunk and walked to the back of the car where Chris stood. She pulled out the bag that contained her dress and showed it to Chris. It was a red satin evening gown with chiffon cuffs across the top. The zipper was in the back. It had slits that come up the calf on the right.

"Hey, not bad! I can't wait to see what you're going to look like in it."

"I tried it on and I think I look ok in it. Nadine didn't think it was me."

"What does she know? She's always so intolerant. You'll look great, Sharie. I'll bet on it," she said with a confident smile.

"Well, let's get it back to your house," Sharie said. They jumped in the car.

"Did you call your mom, yet?" Chris asked.

"I'm about to right now." She looked in her backpack and looked for her cell phone. When she found it and flipped it open. She dialed her house and her mom answered.

"Hello?"

"Hi Mom. I'm checking in, like you asked."

"Okay, baby. Is everything okay?"

"Yes Mom. Everything's fine."

"Alright, I'll see you when you get here."

"Okay, bye Mom."

"Bye, baby."

She closed her phone and started up the engine then pulled off. They drove in silence each wondering what to say.

Chris broke the silence.

"Did Nadine find out anything about the murder today?"

"Yes and no," Sharie said.

"Yes and no? What does that mean?" Chris said.

"She said she overheard her boss, Mrs. Washington, talking to Detective Rayford," Sharie said.

"Okay," said Chris waiting. "And?"

"Anyway...." Sharie continued, "she said she heard him say that his captain wanted him to go back out to Jade's house to see if he over looked something. If this light ever changes we might catch him. We're only a block away."

~ ~ ~ ~

Rayford headed up the street thinking about what Mrs. Wilson had said. *If Jade was so well loved, why would anyone want to kill her so violently?* He thought about the other case that he was working on that happened the same night that Jade was killed. The young woman was killed in the same fashion as she was. The wound was to the back of the neck and the suspect used the same type of weapon. He came to the corner and continued walking. He observed a red Plymouth Duster that just pulled around the bend. He remembered seeing that same car the night before parked down the street from the crime scene. He noticed the two young girls that were in it and remembered seeing them outside that same night. He walked in between two cars to get their attention, but the car instinctively stopped. He walked over and leaned into the window on Chris's side.

"Hi girls. How are you this afternoon?" He showed them his badge.

"We're fine, Sir," they said in unison.

"Great! Hey, I'm trying to find about a friend of yours' house,

PATRICIA

name's Skyler. Could you tell me where he lives?" Rayford didn't want them to know he had gotten the address from Jade's mother. Maybe if they felt as if they were helping he would gain their trust.

"Sure," Chris spoke up first.

"Just keep straight 'til you reach the corner there. Make a right. His house is almost in the middle of the block," Sharie said.

"Thanks. You've been a great help," he said. "Oh, and by the way, you girls knew the girl that got murdered last night, right?"

"Yes Sir. She was a friend of ours," Sharie said.

"Listen," he pause, "I want you girls to be careful and stay out of trouble. This person who did this is a real psycho. He or she struck again after Jade was killed. The press doesn't have a clue about all this and we want to keep it that way. We don't want to scare the perpetrator off by leaking any information out to the press. Also, here's my card. I want you girls to call me if you remember anything and I may require to speak with both of you later. I need to get your names, addresses and phone numbers so that I can contact you."

They both gave him the information he asked for. Another car pulled up behind them and they had to continue on down the street. He bid them goodbye and moved back to the sidewalk, heading in the direction of Skyler's residence.

Several minutes later Rayford was at the door of Skyler's home. He knocked. A little child's voice answered.

"Who is it?"

"My name is Detective Bradley Rayford. Is your mom or dad home?"

"Yes," came the reply. She opened the door. Little Tammy Drake was an adorable child. She couldn't have been any more than 4 feet tall. Her hair was in braids going back away from her pretty little face. She had on a pink jumper with a white T-shirt and her eyes were bright and cheerful. She smiled. Rayford couldn't help but smile back at her. Mr. Drake came to the door.

"Can I help you?"

"Yes, I'm Officer Bradley Rayford from the 103rd precinct." He offered his hand to the man. "I'd like to come in and ask you some questions about your son, Skyler, is he here by any chance?"Mr. Drake shook the pro-offered hand.

"Yeah, come on in and have a seat." Drake moved away from the door to let him in.

Bradley noticed how huge Drake was. He thought he worked out a lot at the gym; he could tell. He was a brown skinned man and stood about 6'2". His eyes where piercing, as if he could see to the bottom of anyone's soul. His voice was deep and Rayford assumed that he had to have sung baritone in someone's choir at one time or another. He saw Tammy playing on the plush green carpet with her dolls while she watched Barney. She was singing the "I Love You" song, when her father told her to watch TV upstairs.

"Skyler, come down here a minute, Son. There's somebody here to see you," Mr. Drake called out.

"Have a seat detective he'll be down here shortly. What is this all about?" Drake asked.

"There's been a murder, Sir, and I think your son could have some valuable information to our investigation."

"Who was killed?" Mr. Drake couldn't help but feel concerned.

Before Rayford could answer, 18-year-old Skyler came down the steps. He was wearing black pants and a white buttoned up cotton shirt. His hair was corn rowed going back from his forehead to the back of his neck. He wore a black dew rag that tied in the back to keep his hair neat for school the next day.

"Sky, this is Detective Rayford. He wants to ask you some questions, Son." Skyler shook his hand.

"How are you, Sir?"

"I'm fine, young man," Rayford said as he stood up to shake his hand, then they both say down.

"Skyler, do you happen to know of a young girl named Jade Wilson?"

"Yes sir, she's my girl."

"What does this have to with my son, Detective?" his father interjected. Rayford ignored his question.

"I'm sorry to tell you, son, but your girlfriend Jade was murdered last night out side of her house."

Skyler fell down into the chair in disbelief.

"What? How?"

"She was killed with what seems like a hunting knife."

"Oh, God!" he screamed as the tears formed in his eyes. His father got up from the couch where he and Rayford sat, Drake sat down next to his son and held him.

"Someone else was killed about an hour or so later after Jade," Rayford said. "Skyler I know you must be hurting now, but I need to ask you some questions."

"Okay," he said sobbing, nodding his head.

"Did you see her the night that she was killed?" Rayford asked.

"No Sir, my parents and I went away to Cape Cod for a few days on vacation. But I did see her the day before we left."

"And what happened? Did she seem odd to you or act in an unusual way?"

"No Sir. As a matter of fact, her and I had an argument earlier that day."

"Oh? May I ask about what?" He cried more when he thought of the ridiculous argument.

"I was angry with her because I thought she was trying to embarrass me in front of everyone in our math class. I failed my math test and Jade got an A on her's. She made a remark about my grade. She said something like, 'you could have done better,' and everybody heard it and started calling me names. I was so angry, that after school when I walked her to her dance class I told her she could have waited to tell me that when we were alone. She tried to apologize and said she was trying to help, but I wouldn't listen. I know she didn't mean any harm by what she said, but I felt like a fool. Oh God, I feel so bad. I tried to call her the next day to tell her I was sorry for the way I acted, but she wasn't home."

"I see," said Rayford. He felt sorry for the boy, but he knew he couldn't let his emotions get involved. He turned to Drake. "Sir, would you mind if I have a look around in Skyler's room?"

"You think my son had something to do with this?" Drake said angrily.

"Mr. Drake, it is my job to check out everything and everyone. I alone are not at liberty to accuse anyone at this time."

"My son had nothing to do with this you hear me!"

"And I believe you Sir, but I have to do my job!" he said adamantly. Drake paused and thought about it for a moment.

"I'm sorry. His room is upstairs to your left," he said.

Rayford proceeded up the stairs and hung a left. He opened the door and saw that Skyler's room was plastered with posters of famous good-looking singers and actresses. All of them had black hair, even the Caucasian women. *Hmm* he thought. Rayford continued to look around and saw on his right his trophies that he'd won from playing football and basketball sitting on his dresser next to the picture of Jade. To the left of him were his certificates from the boy scouts and his academic awards.

His room was small but modern. His single bed was in front of the large window. The walls were wall-papered blue with striped blue and white trim that continued around the room. He went into his closet and found nothing but suits and things neatly hung. He checked under his bed and saw some old worn Reebok sneakers and a box. He pulled it out and looked inside. *Pictures just pictures*, he thought. He got up and headed for the door. He saw no reason to continue searching the boy's room. He headed back down stairs where Mr. Drake and Skyler sat on the couch staring out the window.

"Alright, Mr. Drake. Skyler. I'm leaving now."

"Okay, Detective. And again, I'm sorry for that outburst."

"No problem, Mr. Drake. Please give me a call if you have any other information." He handed him his card.

"Alright." Drake stood up.

"It's okay, I'll show myself out. You, gentlemen, have a good day."

"Goodbye, Detective," Mr. Drake said solemnly.

Rockford closed the door and started back to his car thinking about how Mr. Drake got upset. *What was that all about?* he thought.

~ ~ ~ ~

Upstairs in Chris's room, Sharie tried on her dress. Chris marveled at how nice she looked. Chris put her dress on that she had cleaned the week before. It was a Papell boutique velvet and satin purple evening gown.

"Not too daring, but satisfying for you, huh? You look absolutely marvelous girl!" Sharie said trying not to sound jealous.

Both of the girls admired themselves in front of the mirror. They decided to do each other's hair and make up and by the time they were done both looked absolutely gorgeous. It was 5:45 p.m. when Sharie remembered she had to go and see her mother. They walked out of the house. Chris stopped to tell her mom, who was in the kitchen that they were leaving. She kissed her goodbye and left out the front door with Sharie on her heels.

Sharie came home only to find her mother at the dining room table reading her book. She heard the front door close and turned around to see Chris and Sharie standing in front of her.

"Wow! You girls look fantastic! Those guys on the dance floor had better watch out for you two!"

They all giggled while Chris and Sharie danced around to show off their dresses.

Sharie's mother broke in.

"Honey, you have a good time tonight and I want you back at a decent hour, alright?"

"Mom!" she said squealing in disappointment.

"But the dance doesn't start getting good until 12!"

"Decent hour, young lady, and that's final!"

"Okay."

"Damn. Can't have any fricken 'fun!" Sharie said under her breath.

"What was that?" her mother said.

"I said the chicken was done," Sharie said.

Chris whispered in Sharie's ear. "Your mom is so overly protective!"

"I know, but I love her." They snickered and sat in the living room. Sharie waited for Matt to show up, while Chris had left to go back home and wait for James, her date, for the evening.

~ ~ ~ ~

Matt showed up on schedule, Sharie peeked out the window and saw him park in front of her house. Matt got out of his blue 1997 Chevy and walked up the front steps to her house.

"Mom, Matt is here. I'm getting ready to leave!" she said yelling up the stairs.

"Alright baby. Have a great time!"

"Alright!"

"Don't forget to..." The slamming of the front door as she left, cut off her mother's warning.

~ ~ ~ ~

Sharie opened the screen door before Matt could ring the doorbell. He opened the storm door. Sharie beamed with delight and confidence. *Wow*, he thought. She's as beautiful as ever.

He came closer to her and whispered in her ear. "Hey, hot mamma, can I go with you?" he said as he pulled away from her and took her by the hand and led her down the steps. They stopped at the front steps in front of his the car.

Matt was a handsome young man with short black hair that he kept trimmed. He was brown skinned and light brown eyes. He stood somewhat taller than Sharie. His muscular frame and beautiful mind are what attracted Sharie to Matt. They met the year before at a high school basketball game, in which he played forward. He fell in love with her the moment he saw her sitting on the stand cheering for them. After the game, he caught up with her and asked her out.Since then they have been inseperable.

"I got a man!" she said with her hands on her hips, face full with attitude.

"What your man got to do with me?"

"Nothing," she said playfully.

"Nothing, huh? Well, if I was him and I saw you talking to me, I'd punchy in the mouth!" They laughed uncontrollably.

"Punchy? Who is your English teacher?" she said laughing hysterically. They paused. He gently took her in his arms then held her face.

"Well, I guess your man would really be angry with me if he saw me do this." He kissed her gently on the lips. She smiled and melted in his arms.

"Hi Matt."

"Hi baby." He pushed her back tenderly to get a full look of her. "You look wonderful!"

"Thanks. You're looking mighty spiffy yourself in that black tux."

"The reason why I look so good is because I have a beautiful girl with me!" She smiled and kissed him. He pulled away slowly then walked with her to his car and opened the car door for her and said, "Ms. Johnson, your carriage awaits you." She smiled and got in.

CHAPTER 3
THE DANCE

Skyler sat on his bed staring at the dress suit hanging on the back of his closet door. He was still in shock. It was as if a big hole had been ripped through his heart. He couldn't believe that Jade was gone. Looking at the suit reminded him of Jade. She had helped him pick it out to match her silver gown for tonight. He would have picked her up a half-hour ago and be at the dance by now. He debated whether he should still attend without her. He knew she would still want him to go, but it didn't feel right.

Skyler had known Jade ever since junior high school. They had started dating in the eighth grade when she had broken up with an old boyfriend. She had not just been his girlfriend, but she had been his best friend. Skyler thought that he and Jade would go to college, get married and have children together. Jade wanted a dance troop of girls and he wanted a lot of boys so they could have a basketball team. It wasn't going to happen now.

He stood up from the bed feeling like a heavy weight had been placed on him. Skyler needed to go to the bathroom. His head was splitting like a chord of wood. He needed painkillers, heavy duty ones to take away the pain that was in his heart, as well as his head. He stood in front of the sink and looked at his reflection in the mirror on the medicine cabinet. Skyler's eyes were all red and puffy from crying. He almost didn't recognize himself. The last time he had cried this much was when his dog, Trip, had died.

He turned on the faucet and filled the basin with cold water. When it was full he scooped the frigid liquid in his hands and threw it on his face. He repeated that several times before reaching for his big, black, terry cloth towel. Skyler almost started crying again. Jade had given him the towel for his birthday last year with a bunch of other stuff. It was going to be hard with having so much left to remind him of Jade and the life they would have had.

Skyler's father had sat and talked with him for almost an hour consoling him. He told Skyler that he should attend the dance in honor of Jade. All of their friends would be there. Skyler turned on the shower and tested it for the right temperature. It wouldn't wash away his pain, but he needed to take one.

Darnell Drake found today the most difficult in being a father. He had gotten his children away from the ghettos, hoping that they would never have to go through something like this in their lives. He found himself crying softly. He hated to see his son in so much pain. He couldn't imagine what Jade's parents were going through. It would kill him to lose Skyler.

Jade had always been a nice and good girl. Skyler was lucky to have found such a woman so early in his life. Darnell remembered that it took him sometime to find the right woman to marry, when he finally decided to settle down.

It was going to take time for Skyler's wounds to heal. The fact that he and Jade had said cruel words the last time they had spoken was the hard part. He had no doubt that the two young people were in love and destined to marry. He told Skyler that he should still go to the dance in memory of Jade. All their friends would be there and they would be better support for him right now. He had heard his son enter the shower and prayed that he had changed his mind about the dance.

~ ~ ~ ~

Sharie, Matt, Chris and James had arrived at the dance hall finding the place alive with teens their age dancing to the latest hip-hop songs. Everyone was there, except Nadine and Nicole. Sharie thought they would show up late as usual, just so that Nadine could make her grand entrance.

Chris pointed out Mr. Brinkley, their history teacher.

"There's Mr. B. He always looks so creepy. Didn't anyone ever teach him how to dress? That suit is so Retro seventies."

"Yeah," Sharie agreed with her friend as Matt stood there watching the crowd.

"You remember he used to give Jade a hard time in class. He would always pick on her whenever he thought she wasn't paying attention, when in all actuality she was way ahead of him and she never let him forget it. He hated that she knew more about history than he did. He was going to give her an 'F,' but Mr. Jamison found out that he was doing it on purpose." The group walked a little further into the crowd and greeted some of their classmates.

"There's Mr. Jamison," Chris whispered capriciously. Everyone knew she had a crush on the man including Jamison. "Now, that's what I call a man. Look at that suit. He really knows how to fill out those pants."

James pinched Chris and said, "Now look who's talking."

"Well, he does look good for an old head," Chris said playfully

"Chris, get your mind out of the gutter. Jamison couldn't date you even if he wanted to," Matt chided her.

"Oh, come on Matt," Sharie interfered. "There's nothing wrong with an older man and a younger woman. You are older than me."

"Only by six months, not a decade. The man is ancient," Matt continued. He chuckled.

"Well, I think he's a nice man and I would date him if you weren't around," Sharie confessed with a puppy dog look in her eyes .Matt rolled his eyes and led Sharie to the dance floor.

"We'll be right back."

Chris had been standing with James for about five minutes when he left to get some refreshments. Out of nowhere, Brinkley approached her from behind.

"Hello, Miss Jones. Would you like to dance?"

Paul Brinkley was a short plump man with short brown hair that began receding. Brinkley's hair was always jelled back and parted to the right. He kept his black 1960's nerdy glasses taped together in the middle, which covered his hazel eyes. He had been meaning to get another pair of glasses, but somehow it would always get lost in his other everyday activities. He stood there a moment in his gray plaid suit with blue stripes and blue bow tie licking his cigarette stained teeth, that protruded over his bottom lip, looking at Chris. Chris's head whipped around to acknowledge Brinkley.

"You've got to be kidding, you pervert! I wouldn't dance with you if you were the last teacher on earth!"

Brinkley seemed to be upset with Chris's reaction and went to take a step backwards. There was no telling what she was going to do. He only had the best intentions since she was not dancing with anyone.

"Sorry, I just thought you'd like to dance."

"I will dance when I am ready, besides I'm here with James. Plus Mr. Jamison promised me a dance so you can move on to the next wall flower." Chris gave him a look that could have killed. The girl didn't want him anywhere near her so he walked away without saying another word.

~ ~ ~ ~

Darnell called up to his son when he heard the door to his room slam shut.

"Skyler, are you getting dressed for the dance?"Skyler heard his father's inquiry and yelled his response back.

"Yeah, I'll be ready in five minutes."

When Skyler finally came down stairs he stood in front of his father, who was sitting on the couch watching television.

"You look good, Sky."

"Thanks pop. I still hate wearing ties, but it goes with the suit."

"Just think, Jade is watching you from heaven so I think you can deal with it for one night."

"I guess so." Darnell lifted a set of keys in his hand and shook them.

"I want you to take the BMW tonight and be careful."

"Thanks. I will be, Dad." Skyler took the keys and headed for the front door. Tammy came running into the living room screaming his name.

"Skyler don't forget this."Tammy was carrying the corsage that he had gotten for Jade and the carnation that he was supposed to wear. He stopped to let her hand it to him.

"Thanks Sis. I forgot all about them." He kissed his sister on the cheek and left the house.

~ ~ ~ ~

When Skyler reached the dance hall he left the flowers in the car and walked to the entrance. At the door he saw all his friends and classmates having a good time. He saw Chris flirting with another boy while her date was not looking.

"Hey, Chris," Skyler announced.

"Hey. How ya' doin'?" Chris said knowing it was Skyler's voice coming from behind her.

"I'm doing okay." Skyler hugged her. "How are you holding out?"

"I'm doing good," she said stepping out of his embrace and looking into his eyes. They were still a little puffy, but that was expected.

"I feel like I'm in the *Twilight Zone*. Did you hear anymore about the case?"

"No, but we did bump into Detective Rayford, the one in charge of the investigation, before we got here."

"Did he say anything?"

"All he wanted to know was where you lived."

"Yeah, he came by the house and told me. We just got back home this morning. I didn't know. I hope they find that sicko. Did you talk to Jade's Mom?"

"Yes, briefly and she was still crying. I told her if there was anything that I could do, please call us."

"Jade had left a message on my answering machine that said she was sorry and to meet her tonight and I thought everything was okay. I still can't believe it."

"It wasn't your fault."

"I should have been there to walk her home. I could have picked her up in the car and then she wouldn't have been on the streets by herself."

"Don't think like that Sky. You weren't even here."

"I know. My father talked to me about guilt and told me that it wasn't my fault. He was the one who persuaded me to come to the dance. You should have seen Tammy. She was so excited, that she got the flower I had bought for Jade. We didn't tell Tammy yet. She wanted to know why the police were at our house. My dad will explain it to her better."

Chris was at the verge of tears listening to Skyler, but she managed to hold them back.

"Who where you talking to before I walked over?"

"Oh, that was Shawn. He just wanted to dance that's all."

"Oh, I see. Chris, you're never going to change are you?" Skyler asked with a look of concern on his face.

"Hey, you know me. There's too many fish in the sea and I have to catch more than one to keep me on my toes, you know what I mean?" she said laughing. Skyler couldn't help but laugh with her.

"Well, why don't we go out there and shake some booty?"Skyler suggested.

"I'm with you, boss."

Chris and Skyler began dancing next to Sharie and Mark. The couples changed partners a few times until the band took a break. Ashley, the lead singer of the band, walked over to Skyler and his group.

"Sky, sorry to hear about Jade. You know I'm going to miss her," Ashley said with a sorrowful look in her eyes.

"Thanks Ashley. I appreciate it,"Skyler replied.

"Is there a song you want to hear tonight?"

"Can you do 'On the Wings of Love'?"

"For you Sky, anything. I'll tell Jake. He'll be glad to do it. Jade always liked his piano playing." "Thanks again."

"Don't mention it."

Ashley went back to the band and told Jake about the request. Jake was more than happy to do Jade's favorite song. The sound of the microphone squealed as Ashley took it in her hand.

"Everyone, we lost a great classmate and friend. We are doing 'On the Wings of Love' in the memory of Jade Wilson. Here's to Jade." The band cued in and started the song. Chris and James started dancing right where they were, while Sharie and Mark went back on the dance floor. Skyler stood at the refreshment table trying not to get too emotional. Jade did love this song and wanted it to be their wedding song.

Chris was in heaven or at least for the moment. She loved dancing with James, the love of her life. He couldn't think of anything to say to her so he decided to talk about Jade

"Chris, I am sorry to hear about Jade. I commend you for coming to the dance despite your lost." Chris looked up at him and glowed inside.

"I'm going to miss her, but we all promised to be here no matter what." She put her head on his chest as they sway to the music.

"James, can I ask you a question?"

"Sure, Honey," James said.

"Do you think we'll ever be as close as Jade and Skyler were?"she asked with love and compassion in her voice.

"Well, I thought we were," he said.

"We are," she said. "But I don't ever want us to break up, or leave each other angry. I hope we stay together forever,"she said. He took her face in his hands and gently kissed her.

"I don't plan on going anywhere, baby."

"Me neither," she said as they continued dancing.

Paul Brinkley stood at the refreshment table pouring a cup of punch, when he happened to be looking onto the dance floor. Little Miss Chris Jones and James on the dance floor together. He saw James touch her face. Maybe the girl was crying; she did just lose one of her best friends. *Humph, if not I'll deal with that punk in due time*, he thought.

CHAPTER 4
THE PLOT THICKENS

It was getting late when Doctor Judith Van-Helving, the 103rd precinct's forensic pathologist, started the autopsy on Jade Wilson. She turned on the dictaphone to begin the dictation of the autopsy report and removed the white sheet that covered the young woman's body. In all her years as a forensic pathologist and as a medical examiner, she could not determine why someone would do something as terrible as this. She immediately notices the lacerations on her neck and fingers. She adjusted the overhead lighting for a better view. Turning Jade's neck, she discovered the revolting wound made by the hunting knife.

With obvious signs of struggle, Judith finds animal and clothing fibers underneath Jade's nails. The right index fingernail was broken to the cuticle and covered with dried blood. Turning her neck, she could see the obvious trauma where the knife went through. She continued to look for more evidence for the police to prosecute the perpetrator. While examining the back of her neck further, she made a prediction of what size the knife could have been. She took out a ruler to measure the length of the wound, which turned out to be three inches lengthwise and two inches horizontally. She then stood to the side of the body to lift it to one side looking for other bruising or markings, but none were found. While examining the body, she heard the door to the morgue open and noticed Detective Rayford standing in the doorway. She turned around and looked up at him over the top of her glasses.

"Excuse me, can I help you?"

"Yes. I'm Detective Rayford with the 103rd district."

"Oh, well, come in Detective. What can I help you with?"

"Doctor, I was hoping that you could enlighten me with information concerning the deceased woman that you happen to be examining," Rayford started.

"Well, besides the fact that the knife wound was the cause of death, I found animal and clothing fibers under her nails. I took a blood culture of the dried blood that was under her nails and sent them down for DNA testing. The test came back that Ms. Wilson was B positive and there were no other blood types found. When I heard that Ms Wilson was B positive, it made me think of my daughter, Sarah." Rayford looked at her oddly. *Ok, she's a little strange*, he thought.

"I'm sorry to hear that ma'am. How old is your daughter?"

"She would have been seventeen, but she died in a tragic car crash a few years ago."

"Again, I'm sorry to hear about your lost." He paused for a moment. "You said you found animal and clothing fibers?"

"Yes, sure did."

"Could you tell me where those fibers could have come from?"

"Hold on a second." Judith took the samples that she laid on her desk and put them under the microscope once more. She adjusted the lens to get a better look of her findings, coming to the conclusion that the fibers could have come from a leather coat, preferably black. She told her findings to Detective Rayford.

"Hmm, black leather huh?"

"Yes. That's what it looks like."

"Was there anything specific about the fibers that you found, other than it could have come from a black leather jacket?"

"No. None that I could find," she said.

"What about the wound?"

"It looks as if it could have come from a hunting knife as you described in your report. The length of the knife had to be approximately three inches in diameter and two inches long."

Rayford pulled out the plastic bag that he bought with him and handed it to the doctor. "I found this earlier back at the crime scene. I was wondering if you could examine this as well. I believe it came from the perpetrators pants or coat of some kind." Judith took the bag and emptied its contents then she immediately placed it under the microscope.

"There seems to be some blood on the back of the button near the hole. It's a microscopic drop of blood, but it is present. I will try to match it with the blood sample that I found on the knife to see if it matches Ms. Wilson's blood type or the blood that I found under her nails."

~ ~ ~ ~

An hour had pasted as they waited for the test results to come back. Rayford noticed how very attractive the doctor was. He thought she reminded him of his girlfriend in college.

Dr. Van-Helving stood 5'8" possibly 155 lbs. She was in perfect shape, jogging faithfully each morning before heading out to work. She was a strict vegetarian and always tried to find new ways to take better care of herself. Judith's hair was auburn, which she kept in a bun and only let it down when she was relaxing at home. Like most days, she wore her white hospital coat with her stethoscope wrapped around her neck. Judith had the sexiest baby blue eyes Rayford ever saw, yet he'd never tell her or his wife. She had the face of a model and her skin was as smooth as a baby's bottom. The phone rang distracting his thoughts.

It was Jake Dumas, Doctor Van-Helving's assistant, on the phone. The results were in. Judith and Rayford left to pick the reports up. When they returned she compared the test results and came to the conclusion that all of the samples came from one person the perpetrator. Jade's blood type was B positive, while the samples where A positive. She shared the results with Rayford.

"Hmm, well, okay ma'am. Thanks for your help. I'll let you return back to your work."

"Anytime, Detective," she said with friendly smile.

~ ~ ~ ~

Nicole and Nadine had arrived at the dance late with their dates. Nicole wore a pink full-length gown with a beautifully embellished two-piece design that flattered her in every way. The jacket she wore had a detachable collar and cuffs for the added versatility. Her skirt was flat in the front with side elastic insets with back-zip closure.

Nadine came to the dance dressed as if she where about to go to a formal wedding in a black floor length dress that seemed to hug her every curve with long sleeves and a V-neck beaded jacket with a one button closure. Her dress had a scalloped neckline. She wore her hair in a French twist with curls dangling on both sides of her temples; her makeup was unblemished.

Every male in the room paused to stare as they made their entrance. Most girls cocked their heads and rolled their eyes. Some even slapped their dates for staring for too long. Nadine and Nicole stopped to look at themselves, smiling and giving each other a high five.

"When you got it you got it," Nadine said.

"What can you do?" Nicole replied as she shrugged her shoulders, then pointed up with her hands to the ceiling. They both laughed. They spotted their friends and their dates at a table eating and drinking punch.

James finally emerged from the bathroom again and sat next to Chris.

"Whew, too much punch," James said.

"You sure you're ok?" asked Chris.

"I'm fine, baby. Just got to lay off the juice that's all."

"Okay, if you say so."

Nadine and Nicole arrived at the table. "Hey guys."

"Oh so, you finally made it, huh? Dateless as usual?" Skyler spoke up.

"Oh shut up, asshole! Don't start in on me. Mark is outside parking the car and Nicole's guy went away for the weekend. Nicole can never be on time for anything."

"That's not true!" shot back Nicole.

"Yeah, okay. Whatever you say, girl," came Nadine's reply. Mark finally came in and he kissed Nadine.

"Hey baby, are these people given' you a hard time?" He turned to look at the crew at the table then pulled out a chair for Nadine. Skyler did the same for Nicole. James started to move to help the ladies with their seats, but he saw the other guys had everything under control.

"Please! These young'ns can't handle me!" Nadine said.

"Shut up, girl, and sit the hell down!" Chris said yelling.

They all sat quietly for a few minutes until Nadine broke the silence.

"Hey, check this out. Has anybody heard about the new fun house that's supposed to open this summer?" asked Nadine.

"Yeah, I have," said Sharie. "What about it?"

"Well, I say why don't we go and check it out? You know.... have a little fun after we blow this joint tonight," Nadine said.

"Girl, are you crazy or just plain stupid?" asked Sharie. She contiued, "Don't you know there's a maniac on the loose? Come on! Jade is gone! Hello?"

"Oh please, Mrs. Holier than thou! I know about the murderer and I'm sure Jade wouldn't pass up an opportunity like this. Look, I'm not trying to be insensitive here, she was my friend too. I'll miss her terribly just like the rest of you, but I know Jade would want us to go. She was a fun person and a little daring, you guys know that. Besides, we know the guy that runs the place and he could let us in to take a peek for a little while. You all know Mr. Sams, the hot dog venderoutside the school?"

"I know him," Nicole acknowledged. "But I know I wouldn't buy a hot dog off of him anymore. Shoot gave me the runs for days!"

"Ewwwww!" They all said in unison and laughed.

"Girl, that's information you could have kept to yourself!"said Chris.

"Anyway, he told me he'll be working there this summer part time and he has the keys to the fun house. Look, I heard that the place has some really spooky stuff in there. Now is anybody going with me or not?" Nadine said, arms folded with an attitude.

"My question is, will Mr. Sams stay there with us the entire time and will the guys here go with us?"said Sharie. Skyler said nothing, but looked intrigued. Mark seemed interested.

"Of course Sams will be there. He told me that he had to do some cleaning in there tonight and he would let us come in and take a look around. I'm sure by the look on the guys' faces they will come. Right guys?" said Nadine. Both guys nodded in agreement.

"Hey, why don't we ask Jasmine if she wants to come? She's right over there with Mr. Brinkley," Nicole said.

"Hey Brinkley! Back up, and stop trying to rob the cradle you pervert!" screamed Nadine.   Brinkley turned from Jasmine and gave Nadine a look of annoyance.

"OOOOOOhhhh. I'm so scared!" Nadine shot back at him.

"Little girl, you'd better make sure you show up for class and pass my test next week or you WILL be scared!" he yelled back.

Jasmine laughed at her from across the floor while Nadine's fellow comrades laughed, but when she turned around to face them they tried to be quiet with silly smirks on their faces. Nicole got up from the table and moved across the floor to pull Jasmine away from Brinkley to ask her if she wanted to join them in there little after the dance adventure. She agreed and Jasmine went back to her table to inform her boyfriend that she would be leaving with Nicole and the rest of them. Mark danced with Nadine while James took Chris back on the dance floor. Skyler asked Sharie to join him for one more dance. Nicole danced with Matt.

Brinkley some how got wind of the teens after dance activities and sat near the entrance alone. His hands folded as he stared out into space. He thought it would be quite motivating to follow the bunch of hooligans, as he called them. He thought of an explanation to tell everyone and headed for his car and waited for the group to come out.

Jasmine hopped in the backseat of Nadine's car while Nadine sat on the passenger side as Mark attempted to start the engine. James and Chris were parked in front of them. Mark saw Chris and James get in the car and rev up the engine. He watched the back taillights come on as James pulled out from his parking space. Sharie, Matt and Nicole were parked too far up the street for Mark to see them pull out.

The temperature began to drop down in the teens as snow flurries began. The condensation from everyone's breath in the car started to fog up the windows. Pulling out his handkerchief, Matt wiped the driver side window. Putting the key into the ignition Matt started the car. He pulled up behind James and Chris; however, Nadine had suggested that they go around them.

Nadine was the only one that knew the way to the fun house. She didn't appreciate Mark taking the keys from her and jumping in her car as if it were his. She thought she'd let him have it later when they were alone. She didn't like anybody telling her what to do or anyone taking control of her belongings. She often thought of herself as a strong-willed person; a leader, never a follower like some of her friends. She had to be in the thick of things and always running the show. Nadine liked being in the spotlight; the object of everyone's attention. Being in the background was not her forte'.

Nadine turned and glanced at Mark, giving him a look of contempt, but she knew deep down in her heart that she loved him. She was angry and wanted to have it out with him at that very moment.

Mark turned and noticed that Nadine was staring at him like she wanted to punch his lights out. "What's wrong?"

"Nothing!"she lied.

"Don't give me that crap, Nadine. I know when there's something wrong with you. I know you and I…" Nadine cut him off.

"Well, you think you know me, but anyway, I don't want to talk about it. Just shut the hell up and drive!"

Jasmine cut in. "Hmm, a little testy tonight. Aren't we?"

"Shut up!" Nadine snapped.

Mark just shook his head and continued to drive. He gave up a long time ago on figuring his girl out, but he knew for sure that he loved her. He loved her for her vivaciousness and the fact that she was smart, and because he knew how much she loved him in return. Even though at times like this he wondered where her true affection lay. He was now approaching the intersection of Stenton Ave and Washington Lane.

"Which way, Nadine?" asked Mark.

"Just keep straight down Washington Lane and hang a left on Woolston Street," Nadine said still fuming a little. She decided to break the tension and bent down to turn on the radio. The song 'Thriller' by Michael Jackson came on. Nadine and Jasmine began seat dancing while Mark looked at them from his peripheral vision.

"Turn that up, girl! That's my song!" came Jasmine.

Mark continued to drive down the tree-lined street. He glanced in his rear view mirror for a moment as he turned down Woolston Street. He could have sworn he saw another car turn behind Sharie's car. It looked to him as if Brinkley's car was behind her, but he couldn't make out his face from such a distance. He ignored it and continued on while Nadine and Jasmine unrelentingly sang and seat danced around him.

"How much further?" Mark insisted.

"A few more blocks!" she screamed over top of the music blaring.

As they approached, the fun house came into view. Nadine and Jasmine stopped with their shenanigans and took in the view of the place they where about to enter. From a side view they could see the top of the clowns red hair that sat in the middle of the entrance to the fun house. As they all got closer Mark found a parking space as did Skyler, Sharie, Matt, Chris, James and Nicole. They got out of their cars and walked over through the gravel-covered ground.

The area was open, surrounded by thick shrubbery and trees. Not too far away in back of the fun house was an old cemetery. The moonlight shimmered amongst the head stones while eerie sounds of night creatures could be heard in the distance. They stood in awe of the old place and realized that it had to have been closed for several years. Everyone noticed the rusty, old wooden railing that was in need of repair. It was once painted white and it ran around the entire building. In the middle was the ticket window that was also wooden and capped with wooden planks that covered the ceiling. It looked like it belonged on the top of someone's home. A few stairs stood on the side of the ticket window while the broken door was to the immediate right. Wooden beams surrounded the structure. The outside walls were painted a dingy red. Over top of the ticket window was a sign that read *Ocean River Fun House*. Under that was another sign that looked like someone tried to scratch out in blood with a sharp instrument. It said *Enter at Your Own Risk*.

Sharie and Nicole felt very intimidated about the whole scene.

They contemplated about leaving, but didn't want their friends to make fun of them. Everyone was cautious about entering the rickety old place, except Nadine and Chris. They where ready for action. Sharie, on the other hand ,was just as skeptical as the rest of her other friends. She looked for reassurance from Matt. He gave it to her. They entered not knowing someone was hiding among the bushes in back of them.

CHAPTER 5
THE DEMISE OF ANOTHER

Detective Rayford returned to the precinct not knowing what else to do. He sat at his desk glancing through old mug shots of other suspected serial killers and unsolved cases on his computer. He searched for blood types and fingerprints that were printed under each person's file. *Dammit, were are those damn reports from forensics? What are they? Complete freaking idiots down there or what? My God, those fucking people are so slow! I must have some answers and I need them now!* Rayford thought. He turned to the left picked up the phone and dialed the forensics office.

A woman's voice came on the other line, "Forensics, how can I help you?"

"Yeah, this is Detective Rayford. Get me Dr. Van-Helving." He held his temper and waited. The woman came back on the line again.

"I'm sorry Detective, but Dr. Van-Helving just stepped out. Could I take a message?" the woman informed him.

Rayford sat fuming. "Get me somebody else in forensics."

"One moment, Sir."

After a short delay a male voice came over the receiver, "Jake here, how can I help you Detective?"

"Listen, Dammit! I've been waiting forever for some damn answers about the button I had sent down to you guys the other day. What the hell is going on? You people are trying my patience and trust me you don't want to mess with me, ok? Now tell me, what did you find?"

"Hold your horses their buddy. You're angry with the wrong fella here!" Jake recognized frustration, but tried to remain calm while speaking to the detective.

"Hold my horses? You've got to be out of your fucking mind! You listen to me, you stupid ass imbecile! You…"

"Okay, Okay!" Jake said sternly. "Here's what we've got. It seems your perpetrator has never been arrested before so we can't make a match on the blood type or the prints that you gave us. We did, however, find something that you may think is strange."

"Oh really. Amuse me, would ya?"

"I can't understand why Dr. Van-Helving didn't tell you this before, but at the time of Ms. Wilson's death, she was two months pregnant."

"What? You're kidding me, right?"

"Nope."

"Ya know what? Somebody is not being honest with me and I know who it is. Thanks pal."

"Sure thing, asshole!" Jake finally had it with this Detective Rayford and ended the conversation.

The line went dead. Rayford slammed the phone down.

"Got to make a note of that jack ass hanging up on me!" he said out loud. He lay back in his chair and ran his hands through his long black hair in disgust. He could feel a migraine coming on. *Skyler is lying to me and I'm going to find out why,* he thought. He also remembered something Jade's parents told him about Mr. Brinkley, the history teacher. They told him about the rumor of how badly he treated Jade from his first interview with them. He decided to take a trip to the school in the morning, then go and see Skyler.

~ ~ ~ ~

The inside of the Ocean River Fun House was just as creepy as the outside. Mr. Sams met up with the group of teens. He unlocked the door, then he told them he couldn't stay, that his wife was at home sick with the flu. He said he'd stay for a few minutes to get some of his tools he'd left two weeks ago in the basement.

Sams and Nadine were the first to enter with Mark on their heels. Sams left the group to find his stuff. Chris went in after James with Skyler right behind them. It was Skyler who thought of how cool the place must have been when it was in operation. Nadine walked in without fear holding Mark's hand. In fact, she was excited about it all. Jasmine clung to Mark's shirt. From the entrance the crew could see that the place was dark. Only the light from the moon had shone through a hole in the ceiling. The place reeked of foul urine that someone left years before.

Further inside to the right was the hall of glass. Nadine wished her and her friends had gone back home to change. Her feet were killing her and she knew her girlfriends had to have felt the same as she did. The gang moved further into the dank dark place and through the glass maze. Sharie stopped and called everyone's attention.

"Everybody listen up a sec, why don't we make this more interesting, and split up?"

"I don't believe it!" Chris replied emphatically. "Mrs. Passive wants to live on the edge for once in her life!"

"Shut up, Chris!" Sharie said. They laughed for a few moments and decided to split up after all.

"Okay, you guys. We'll meet back at the front door in 20 minutes. This place gives me the creeps and I want to get out of here," said Sharie.

"You are just too petrified all the time, Sharie. You need to get over that and live a little like me," Nadine said.

"Oh no. You didn't just say that!" Chris said, with her hand on her hips snapping her fingers and neck with attitude.

"What are you talking about?" Nadine pretended that she didn't say anything wrong. Chris paused and smirked at what she was thinking.

"I remember, at Halloween, when we went trick or treating and that guy was dressed in a corny zombie suit remember? He jumped out of the coffin that was standing up on his porch and you wouldn't go and get the candy! Remember that? Do you remember when he popped open the coffin and YOU were so scared that you took off down the street like a bat out of hell crying…"

"Okay, so I'm not so brave all the time, geez, give me a break here would ya! Everyone started to laugh, but Nadine shot all of them a glance that quickly made them change their minds and muffled their laughs. Nadine grabbed and pulled Mark's hand dragging him down the hall mumbling under her breath.

Jasmine and Nicole followed behind them, while Sharie, James, Skyler, Chris and Matt went to the immediate right. It was cold inside the complex. Chris wished she had brought her jacket, sweater or something. She and her friends noticed how dirty the floors were with trash strewn around; mice and rats could be seen from time to time throughout the filthy place. Spiders and cobwebs hung from the ceiling, while huge water bugs scattered across the floor. A few of the bugs flew around them. Sharie and the girls screamed and ducked trying to avoid them. Sounds of a dripping faucet could be heard in the distance. They were trapped inside the maze.

Somehow Chris got away from James and her friends, and suddenly found herself alone. She could see her friends wandering all around her. She kept telling herself that she wasn't afraid and that she would catch up to them. She saw an exit and went through, but to her demise it was just another glass wall. Chris thought she heard someone behind her. She turned and found no one, but in the reflection on the glass was a figure of a gruesome man with a black top hat on. His face was revealed through the light from the reflection of the glass that quickly passed over his grotesque face. Without her knowledge, he stood behind her and reached for what he thought would be his next victim. All he caught was air. Chris turned again. She started to feel a little edgy and by this time she wanted to get out. She got tired of running into a dead end. She saw Skyler and banged on the glass.

"Skyler! Over here! Help me. I can't get out!" Skyler thought he heard something and turned to look, but didn't pay it any mind.

"Skyler! Stop fucking playing, man, and help me get out! I'm serious!" she shouted, continuing to bang on the glass for a moment then gave up after she saw Skyler leave the area.

Chris turned and lay on the glass, arms folded, with disgust written all over her face. She sighed and continued to walk down the hall. She was determined to get out one-way or the other. She saw another opening on the left and went that way. She could see the exit sign on the other side of the glass. She turned that way and finally got out. Chris found herself walking through an old rusty circular moving tunnel. As she went through it, it unexpectedly turned on. She screamed as she waddled through.

"Who the fuck turned this shit on?" she shouted. "Nadine, if you did this, so help me God. I'm going to kick your ass when I get out of here! It's not funny, man!" Chris fell as she got out of the tunnel and banged her knee hard on the dirty cold floor. She swore again then got up off of the floor. Her knee hurt a little but she managed to get to a door. She heard voices and swung open the door.

"Nadine! You bit... oh snap, what the hell is this?" The room she had opened was dim. She could barely make out what was in front of her hand, let alone what was in the room. She kicked something; cautiously reaching down, and to her surprise it was a flashlight. She turned it on and was happy that it still had some life in it.

She scanned the room. The room was made into an old funeral home it was eerie with cobwebs all over the old walls and in between the beams and the ceiling. The coffins that were placed strategically around the room were covered with dusty molded white sheets. As she went inside the smell of death was in the air. Curiosity got the best of her for some strange reason. She focused the flashlight to the right and saw a skeleton hanging from the ceiling. Jesus, you think these people could've come up with better props? she thought. Even she had to chuckle at that. She continued surveying the room where the skeleton hung. She moved the flashlight down. To her horror, she found another skeleton, but this one had flesh still on it as if it died just a few days ago! The skeleton was dressed in surgeon's uniform, flies and maggots engulfed its body, blood covered its uniform. In fea,r she stood and looked at the face of the skull with one eye still attached to it. The other eye had a maggot crawling out of it.

Chris felt her stomach churning. She wanted to up chuck right there, but she managed to hold it in. She took the flash light and moved it further down to reveal a female mannequin with her head severed. Chris screamed and scurried a few steps back, only to find another dead body slumped in the corner behind her. She turned to look, it was Mr. Sams. He still had his screwdriver, except it wasn't in his hand. It was embedded in his right eye; blood oozed out from it. Chris screamed, and ran to find her way out.

~ ~ ~ ~

Nadine and the rest of the crew found each other stuck in the basement. They stumbled upon the basement area while trying to get out of the walls of glass.

"Who's dumb idea was it to make that left turn at Albuquerque?" exclaimed Nadine. No one laughed at her pitiful attempt to break out in a joke. Everyone was scared and worried, since no one saw Chris in the past few minutes. James had gone off to look for her, but didn't return yet.

"Damn. What is taking James so long to find Chris?" Sharie said.

"I don't know, but I know one thing. This place is totally freaking me out and I'm ready to roll up outta here," Nicole said. Nadine broke in.

"You two are getting on my last nerves with all this spooky crap! Chris is fine. James is fine. Every freaking body is fine! Okay! So, quit with your yapping. Let's find our way out of here and get back home. My feet are killing me!"

"It seems to me that YOU were the one that wanted to come out here in the first place, Mrs. I Gotta Have Some Damn Excitement! If it weren't for you, we'd all be at home in bed in la la land. But noooo. YOU had to drag everybody out here in your mess!" Sharie said angrily.

"Listen Queen Glenda, from the fricken' Wizard of fricken' Oz…," Nadine's smart remark was cut short.

"You guys hold it down for a sec. I think I heard something over there near that other door," said Skyler. Skyler crept closer while everyone else held their breath and watched as he attempted to open the wooden door. The sound was muffled by the light banging from the other side. Skyler had trouble opening the door. He told Mark to look around for something to help jar it open. Mark found a crow bar and handed it to him. They both pushed on the stuck door together until they popped the lock open. Everyone was amazed at what fell out. It was Chris. Her hands and feet where tied up. Her mouth was duct taped shut and her eyes were covered.

"Oh my God, Chris! Are you alright?"asked Nadine. Matt and Skyler quickly untied her and ripped the tape from her mouth.

"I'm fine, but we got to get out of here and I mean NOW!"

"What happened to you?" Nicole said.

"I saw a dead body upstairs in the room that used to be a funeral home! We've got to get out of here! Somebody else is in here besides us!"

"What gave you that idea?" asked Skyler.

"Excuse me! Hello! I did say I saw dead bodies, you idiot! They grabbed me from behind after I bumped into another dead body! I couldn't see them. They drugged me with a shot of some kind and I slid down into that closet." Mark went back over to the closet and examined it. Indeed there was an opening in the ceiling.

"Where's James?" Chris asked.

"We don't know. He went looking for you and we haven't seen him since,"said Nicole.

"Oh no! Whoever is out there, they're going to kill him and us. I know it! He's killed two other people!" Chris said.

"Two other people? I thought you said there was only one body that you bumped into?" said Nadine.

"No, when I came into the room there was a half dead body dressed in a surgeon's uniform."

"Half dead body? What the hell does that mean? Either it was dead or it wasn't," said Matt.

"No, it was dead. But its flesh was not fully decayed yet. Hello! Who the hell is writing this book? Could you please give this asshole of a character some brains please?"

"You mean to tell me there's a body up there that's still has skin and everything still on it?"

"Ah duh! Yes! And now for the next 65,000 dollar question!" Chris said.

"Okay this is waaaayyy too deep for me. I say let's find James and get the hell outta here!" said Skyler.

"I'm with you man!" Nicole cried out.

~ ~ ~ ~

James wondered back into the walls of glass maze. He wanted to find Chris and hold her in his arms so badly. James and Chris had been going out together for over a year now. He often contemplated about asking Chris's hand in marriage. She was the one he wanted to spend the rest of his life with and he knew it. *I'll ask her tonight*, he thought. But then he thought better of it, because he knew he didn't get her ring paid for yet. He still had two more payments to make on it. He wanted it to be a surprise and this setting was not the place to ask such a romantic question.

As he continued to try to find his way out and find his girl, he thought about her smile, her quirkiness, and her sarcasticness. She was gorgeous; the apple of his eye. She looked so beautiful with the purple flower he had given her earlier. He thought about telling her how much he loved her and wanted to be with her. His mind was quickly turned away from the girl that he loved. He heard something around the corner from where he stood for a moment than continued walking further down the hall and made a right, but was blocked in. He turned left and walked a few more feet seeing the opening. Lying on the ground tied up with a dirty rag in his mouth was Mr. Brinkley. James bent down and quickly untied him.

"Brinkley, what the hell are you doing here?"

"I wanted to see what you pesky kids were up to!" Brinkley coughed and gasped for air. He got up from the musty floor brushing himself off. Brinkley began to speak again, but couldn't. He stood and faced James, suddenly terror filled his eyes as he saw what was behind James. Someone dressed in black with a top hat and clown face took the sound from Brinkley's mouth.

"Speak up man! Com… Aggh!"

The hunting knife plunged into James's head and out through his forehead. Brinkley ducked as the blood from James's forehead squirted and dripped over Brinkley's head and face. Brinkley had the look of horror at the sight of the young man's body being hoisted into the air. His screams went unheard. The sinister man rammed James's body through the other glass behind Brinkley. He squatted as the bodies hurled over him, then fell flat on his back on the floor from the tremendous blow from the victim's and attacker's bodies.

Brinkley got up then ran for his life and prayed he would not be his next victim. The revolting figure bent down while Brinkley ran, and took blood from his victim. He materialized once again in front of Brinkley from out of nowhere. Brinkley, out of sheer horro,r frantically fought for his life. The murderer swung his knife at him. Brinkley dodged the knife and then kicked with all his might at the attacker's hand. The psychotic killer dropped the knife. Brinkley punched him square in his face. It fell back while Brinkley ran hysterically through the glass maze. The executioner gave chase.

~ ~ ~ ~

The crew of teenagers finally found themselves back in the glass maze. Chris couldn't keep her mind off of the whereabouts of her love and friend. They searched and called for James, but to no avail. Chris was determined to find him and she wouldn't leave without him by her side.

"This time we're all staying together. Hold hands everybody." Chris said, leading the group. Everyone made like a chain and held hands as they continued to walk through the maze. They turned left then right and then left again. It was Sharie who saw the body lying on the floor through the glass.

"Oh my God! Chris turn left somebody's lying on the floor!" Sharie screamed.

"Who is it?" cried Chris.

"I don't know. Just turn, Dammit! "

They rushed carefully over the broken glass that lay on the floor. Chris screamed and cried hysterically as she was the first to reach her fallen boyfriend. She almost fell down beside her friend, but Mark and Skyler grabbed her and held her. Skyler turned her face into his chest to block her view of the distorted figure lying on the ground. They dragged Chris and ran through the maze. No sooner than they turned right and headed for the opening to the outside door of the fun house, Brinkley ran into Mark, Skyler, Chris, Nicole, Nadine,

Sharie, Jasmine and Matt. His sudden appearance in front of them made them scream and stare in fright and disbelief.

"Brinkley what the fu..!" Nadine wanted to continue, but he gave her a look that was too serious for words.

"Don't ask questions now we've got to get out of here and..." before he could finish his sentence, the monstrous figure came running towards them with knife in hand. Brinkley tried desperately to open the front door. It was stuck; he kept struggling to open it. Nothing. Everyone screamed with fear.

"What the hell are you doing? Open the fricken' door!" Nadine screamed.

"I'm trying! It's stuck!"

"Oh, my God! Open the freaking door man!" yelled Jasmine.

He banged and pulled. This time it miraculously unlocked, everyone ran out. Sharie and Nadine were the last to run out. The slaughterer grabbed Sharie by her hair. She screamed in terror as he pulled back the knife to stab her. Nadine turned back towards them and decked him in the eye. She saw the killer had dropped the knife. Nadine picked up a hammer that lay by the entrance and commenced to hammer his head in until blood oozed down his face. She grabbed Sharie's arm, then pulled her away. The group ran chaotically for their lives through the open door, down the stairs, and through the entrance to the safety of their cars.

The winter air blew fiercely, around them. The crazed killer ran after them. Force from the air blew its hair back. It paused at the entrance and watched them escape, then it said in a loud shrilling voice, "YOU WILL ALL DIE, YOU WILL ALL DIE!" Its horrifying laughter pierced their ears as they jumped in their cars and sped away.

The fearful gang drove wildly towards the nearest police station. Sharie sat in the car with Skyler and Mark, horrified by what her and her friends just experienced. She sat quietly. Her mind lost and confused. Her body felt numb. She tried to calm herself down, but the events of the night kept her in a state of panic. They were far off from the fun house when Matt, who was in the drivers' seat, spoke up.

"I swear I'll never listen to that crazy Nadine ever again. She brings nothing but trouble. I knew I shouldn't have gone with you guys!"

"Quit your complaining, Matt. What's done is done now, and their ain't nothing we can do about it!" Skyler shrieked.

"How can you say that man? James is dead! If it weren't for Nadine, he'd still be alive! Look at Sharie, hmm? Her mind is gone! That maniac almost killed her as well! And all you can do is sit there and say there nothing we can do about it?"

"What do you want me to say man? Granted, Nadine was a fool for leading us out there. And yeah, she's responsible for this, but what can we do besides get to the police and report what we saw? Besides, nobody twisted your arm to go with us! Punk !"

Matt stopped the car and jumped out. He punched Skyler in the jaw through the open window where Skyler was sitting.

"Oh, see I got your punk ? Get out of the car now! He held his fist up."

Skyler tried to get out to meet his challenger and return his punch. It was Sharie who stopped him. Her senses finally coming back to her.

"Stop it! Just stop it!" she cried.

Skyler sat back down. Matt had the look of anger in his eyes; he wanted to continue with the fight, but thought better of it and jumped back into the driver's seat. Sharie continued.

"Just get back in the car! Stop acting like park apes and think! What would all of your fighting solve, huh? I'm sick and tired of you two pointing fingers! We need to get a hold of that detective that me, Chris and Skyler talked to. I have his card here."

She turned to Matt who settled down now. "Drive down to 8ᵗʰ and Race St. I can see Mark and Nadine behind us, signal for them to pull up next to us," she said.

Matt did as she asked. Nadine drove up next to them. Sharie yelled out the window to Nadine.   "Meet us at 8ᵗʰ and Race. We're headed for the police station down town."

"Alright!" Nadine yelled back.

Sharie could see Jasmine in the back seat, tears streaming down her face while lying on Mark's shoulder for comfort. Nicole sat next to them lost in her own fear.

~ ~ ~ ~

Chris was the first to enter the station. She ran up to the front desk, followed by the rest of the crew. It was Friday night and the station was a buzz with the usual criminals. Drunks, prostitutes, thieves, and other unlawful citizens traveled back and forth with handcuffs on, being led by a policeman or woman dressed in blue. The drunks were rowdier than ever.

Sharie couldn't stand the stench of them as one walked past her. Policemen typing up reports could be herd through out the station. One drunk puked in his cell that was to the left of them further behind the officer's desk. Chris was crazy with emotion when she reached him, exhausted; her body dropped on the small table.

"Officer, we need to speak to Detective Rayford! Is he here by any chance?"

"I must say you look mighty spiffy tonight. What have you kids been up to?" came the officer.

"Listen, Officer..." she looked at his badge for his name, "Kaminski, I have something important to tell Rayford! Is he here or not? We don't have time for your silly questions, alright?"

"Hold on, young lady, what's going on here? Who do you think you are coming in here demanding anything? Where's your respect?"

"I'm sorry, Officer, but I left my respect in my ass while I was running from the scene of a murder!" Chris said sarcastically.

"Rayford is in the back I'll go and get him."

"Thank you!" she said. She mumbled under her breath, "You jerk!"

The officer got up from his desk to get Rayford ,while the crew sat on the bench near the entrance. Ten minutes later, Rayford came out with the officer. He was wearing his black long sleeve turtleneck shirt and jeans. Nadine was the first to see the officer point over to them. She got up, as did the rest of them. He walked over to them.

"You kids wanted to see me?"

"Yes, sir," said Nadine.

"What's the problem?"

"We just came from the abandoned fun house in Mount Airy. My friend's boyfriend was killed, and we found other dead bodies and one of our teacher's was there and nearly got killed!"

"Come over to my desk," Rayford said. All of them followed him back to his desk area. Papers and files were scattered all over his desk. The computer monitor sat to the left, with the keyboard in front of it. Nadine sat next to his desk with her arm supporting her head. Rayford sat down and called the coroner's office. The teens stood and listened to Rayford on the phone.

"Yeah, Rayford. Get me Van-Helving quick! Look, Doc, I need you and your team to get over to the abandon fun house now! I'll meet you over there in about a half hour." He hung up the phone, and then turned to the group in front of him.

"I have all of your phone numbers and I'm calling all of your parents to come and pick you up."

"But we have our cars with us," Sharie said.

"I don't care about that. What I care about is getting you kids safely home. You can come and pick up your cars in the morning."

"Oh great! My mom's going to have a hissy fit when she finds out I'm in a police station! I probably won't see daylight 'till next year!" Nadine said.

CHAPTER 6
THE CHURCH

It was Monday night at First Fellowship Baptist Church. Ashley Jones stood in front of the Mass choir. She held the microphone ready to practice with the choir on the song "How I Got Over." The inside of the sanctuary was considerably large; the brown wooden pews had red cushions on them. The church seats sat to the right and left with the main isle in the middle. Beautiful stained glass windows glowed whenever the sun shown through them on Sunday mornings. A portrait of the pastor hung on the left with another picture of the first lady hung to the right. In the middle, on top of the pictures, was another stained glass window whose view filled the entire back top half of the wall with a yellow stained glass picture of the cross in the middle portion of the sanctuary.

The pulpit stand was covered in red with an emblem of the cross stitched on to the front. Behind the podium, in the middle, was a chair reserved for the pastor that looked as if it were carved out of the wooden wall. The seat inside it had a red cushion. Two medium-sized seats sat on the opposite sides of the pastor's chair. The walls were white with speakers sitting on the wooden archway. On the upper level, were more pews for church visitors to sit. The floors were carpeted red from the two front doors of the church to the altar. In the back of the sanctuary was a table that had offering envelope boxes and other church flyers neatly stacked. Two chairs sat next to the table.

Sister Hattie Mae Brown, the choir director, came from behind the first pew and gestured for the choir to stand. She was a short, heavyset, dark complexion woman with grayish black hair, that she kept in a bun. She looked to be in her early sixties from the wrinkles that began to appear on her face. Her teeth were false, which sometimes slipped out of her mouth whenever she got angry and started yelling.

Hattie Mae's nineteen sixty style-reading glasses usually hung around her neck on pearl beads. Her dress was white with pink flower prints all over it. She loved to wear costume pearl jewelry that she collected over the years. Some were handed down to her from her mother and grandmother. Hattie Mae was a penny pincher and often took her old stockings, cut them down to the knees, then used rubber bands to hold them up and tied them in a ball. She was addicted to big Sunday hats with ornaments adorning it; she tried each week to out do the other women in the church by buying the biggest hat in the thrift store she could find. But on this particular night she decided not to wear one. She felt that was only *for show* on Sundays.

"OK everybody. We have to get this right before service Sunday. Now, I know some of you young folks are upset about the death of Jade, but we have to continue on. Besides, we're singing her favorite song for her this Sunday. Now, Ms. Ashley, you have to sing this song with feeling! With emotion! Do you understand?"

Ashley nodded as she stood with her hands crossed in front of her and her head down.

"Jasmine, PLEASE SING ON KEY!" said Hattie Mae. Hattie Mae turned and started yelling at Deacon Snow who was playing the piano for them. "Deacon Snow, would you please give this chile her note so she can remember it and sing it right!"

"Now, look a here ol' woman, you ain't got to yell at me. I can hear okay?"

Hattie Mae turned to face him, with her hands on her huge hips. "Well, maybe if you'd pay attention sometimes, I wouldn't have to yell atcha! You s'pose to be wearin' your hearin' aid anyways, but ya ol' fool, ya never do!"

Deacon Snow started to get upset by her harsh attitude. "That's 'cause I left'em atcha Momma's house last Sunday when I went vistin'"

"Now hold on Deacon, you aint got no right talkin' 'bout my

momma like that! You know she been dead over fifteen years now! God rest her soul."

"Well, you shouldn't have started in on me 'bout my hearin! I told you I could hear just fine."

"Oh, hush ol' fool, and give the chile her note!"

Deacon Snow played the key for Jasmine, then mumbled another remark under his breath. Hattie Mae rolled her eyes and sucked her teeth, then turned back to face the choir. In her heart of hearts, she truly cared for Deacon Snow, but she never knew how to express her feelings towards him.

She and Snow have been friends for many years and often quarreled a lot. A few times they got into bad arguments, but they always apologized in there own way. They never would actually say the words, 'I'm Sorry,' but somehow they knew.

They were still practicing when Chris, Sharie, Nadine, and Nicole came in the church. All of them took a seat in the back praying amongst themselves when Jasmine saw them come in. She waved catching Hattie Mae's attention.

Hattie Mae turned and saw them sitting back there, began shouting for Deacon Snow to stop the music, which by a miracle he heard her. She faced the girls coming to her and held out her arms to embrace them.

"Nadine, come on up here, 'cause all of ya'll need prayer." Nadine came and everyone in the church said a prayer for them. They thanked the Lord for their safe return and for being unharmed. But they also prayed for the unfortunate victims and their families. "These are some tryin times! I thank you Lord for keeping your arms of protection around these youngins!" said Hattie Mae.

~ ~ ~ ~

Louise Johnson stood over the stove in her red robe and nightgown fixing Sunday breakfast for her family. The wonderful aroma of eggs, sausage, and coffee could be smelled throughout the house. She was still sort of angry with Nadine for going out to the fun house and nearly getting herself killed. But she was happy she was okay.

She moved to the cabinet overhead and pulled out three plates and laid them on the table next to the orange juice and coffee cups. She sat down for a moment still mulling over how to punish Nadine for actions, when Nadine entered the room, still in her night clothes.

"Good mornin' Mom."

"Good mornin' and why aren't you dressed for church yet?"

"Um, because I wasn't planning on going?"

"Oh really, and how did you come to that conclusion, young lady?"

"Mom, please don't start in on me. You know how I feel about church."

"Yeah, I know how you feel about it, but as long as you are under my roof, you will go to church! No if and's or but's about it, young lady. Now march your butt back upstairs and put that dress on that I bought for you last week!"

"Aw man! Come on, Mom!"

"Now! And I'm not playing Nadine."

"Yes, Mom!" She headed out the room towards the stairs, angry.

Louise yelled down the hall to her. "When you're done getting dressed bring your butt back down here and eat your breakfast! And I'm not done talkin to you about last night either young lady!"

"Yes, Mom."

Louise went to the bottom of the steps. "Tell your lazy father to hurry up out of the bathroom so he can eat! I didn't get up at 6 am for nothin'!"

"Alright Mom, dang!"

"Don't 'dang' me, girl! You ain't too old for me to take you over my knee, you know!" Nadine laughed and closed her door. As angry as Louise was with her daughter, she couldn't help but chuckle at the thought of turning her 18-year-old daughter on her knee.

Chris was still asleep when she heard the phone ring next to her on her nightstand. It was Sharie.

"Hello?" she said groggily.

"Girl, you still in the bed?"

"Yeah, and?"

"Come on, Chris. You know we have to sing today. Get up!"

"Okay, Okay, I'm up, damn!"

"I'll meet you at the church, ok? Call Nicole and make sure she's coming too."

"Yeah, okay bye."

"Bye."

~ ~ ~ ~

First Fellowship Baptist Church was alive with spirit when Nadine and her parents entered the church. The Mass choir was singing. Nadine could see Sharie, Chris, Jasmine and Nicole in their appropriate areas in the choir stand. The singers were wearing their new robes. They were bright orange with purple letters that read F.F.B.C. stitched down the right side of their breast. They moved and sang in rhythm to the sound of the drummer and organ player.

Deacon Snow sat with the other members of the deacon board reading the Bible and looking for his passage that he had to read next. Mark sat with his family on the right, while Skyler and his sister and dad sat in the back pew. Nadine and her parents decided to sit in their usual seats, third row from the altar and to the right.

Sister Hattie Mae was standing in the front directing the choir, as usual. She wore her pink dress with flower print and a huge white hat with pink flowers dangling all around it. Her slip was showing a little at the bottom and everyone could see her knee-high stockings being held up with a rubber band and tied in a knot. Everyone was clapping and singing and shouting 'Amen' and 'Hallelujah.'
Nadine was unaffected by the emotions that were going on around her. She sat quietly, while her mom and dad stood up and clapped and sang with the rest of the congregation.

When the choir finished with their selection, everyone sat down. The Reverend Roosevelt Austin Senior approached the podium. He was a tall light complexioned man with white hair that was receding. He looked to be in his early seventies and he spoke with a southern accent. Reverend Austin was a handsome man, and his wife beamed whenever some one would complement him on his looks to her. He turned on his light that sat on the podium and opened his Bible, then began thumbing through the pages and slightly fidgeting. He held the microphone and pulled it closer to his mouth.

"I would like to thank the choir for that wonderful song. They're doing such a great job! Can I get a 'Amen'?"

"Amen!" the crowed replied.

"It's alright to shout sometimes ain't it?"

(Amen!)

"God is such a good God! Am I right about it?"

(Amen!)

"Sometimes you just can't keep still and ahhhh let things ride. You got to get up! And let the world know how good the Lawd has been to ya! Can I get a witness?"

(Amen!)

One woman yelled. "Preach on, Pastor!"

"Amen, amen," said the reverend as he spoke again. "Sister Rose, come on up here." He paused for a moment; the church was quiet ,except for the sound of a baby crying in the back.

"Give her a hand, would ya?"The congregation clapped as the woman approached the platform on the floor in the front.

"First, giving honor to God, Pastor Austin, The Deacons, members and friends. I have the announcements for Sunday December nineteenth. We are sorry to hear of the passing of our church member, Sister Jade Wilson. The viewing will be held here at the church Tuesday night at 7 p.m., followed by the burial at Mount Mariah Cemetery." She looked down at the podium and began to read some of the sympathy cards that were mailed to the church. She paused to turn the pages in front of her, then continued.

"Today, we are out to Second Baptist Church of Franklinville to celebrate their church anniversary. Pastor Austin is asking that everyone attend." She pointed toward each and every one of them in the room. "That means ALL of y'all," she said as she smiled and turned her head back down to her notes. "The pastor is asking that everyone please pay your tithes. Y'all know what the Lord say about that; he said one tenth!" Some people murmured when she said it. "Look it up! He ain't say give me what you can spare! It's in your Bible, read it. Read Malachi third chapter tenth verse and you tell me what it say."

"That's what it say now!" Hattie Mae shouted her agreement.

"Thank you Sista Hattie." Rose said."Now, the building fund. If ya'll want the new air conditioner in here by next summer, we need two hundred dollars more." People began to moan, becoming impatient. "I know y'all don't want to hear that, but guess what? The Lawd said it's going to be ten times hotta in hell! So, could you, please, get your donations in no lata than next week? And last but not least, the Christmas play. We are asking all parents who have children involved in the play to be here at the church no lata than 9 am, so the play won't interfere with devotional service at 11am. Amen?"

"Amen!" several people responded.

"To all our visitors, we here at Fellowship Baptist Church, we welcome you and may the Lawd guide your heart to come again. Thank you." Sister Rose picked up her papers from the podium and returned to her seat, while the congregation clapped.

"Amen." came the pastor, as he came back to the microphone."And now, we will have another selection by the choir."

Sister Hattie Mae got up and directed the choir to stand. She came up to the first mic that was in front of her and spoke into it. "This next song we're about to sing goes out to Sista Jade, 'cause this was her favorite song, and I don't know about y'all, but I know where Sista Jade is! She's somewhere around the throne, praisin the Lawd! This song also goes out to all of her closest friends whom the Lawd saw fit to bring them back to us safe and sound. Amen!"

"Amen!" the people shouted back.

Hattie Mae signaled for Deacon Snow to come and play their song for them. The pastor preached, the church sang, clapped, and shouted in joy. Some danced in the aisles while others remained seated.

Later on that afternoon Deacon Snow, Sister Hattie Mae and a few other church members stayed behind to tidy up the church for Jade's funeral. Deacon Snow went out to the closet to get the vacuum cleaner. Only Sister Rose and Hattie Mae stayed in the sanctuary to polish the wooden pews.

"Hattie Mae, do you know who is the undertaker for Jade's

funeral?"

"No? Who?"

"Chile, they done got that brother in-law of Deacon Snow to do it."

"Oh Lawd! Not him again."

"Yes, they did! I talked to Jade's Aunt last night and she said the same thing. She don't know why her sista went and got that man to do the work either," Rose said.

"Shoot ever' time I think about how he did Sista Mammies daughter, I get angry! He made that chile look like she saw flour befoe' she past! All that white mess all smacked up on that chile's face like that! Don't make any sense! Shoot, look like she just walked right into the flour! POW! You know what I'm sayin?" Hattie Mae gestured how the deceased woman's body walked into the flour. She chuckled and Rose joined in.

"Well, hopefully, Lawd willin,' he won't do such a bad job," Rose said.

"I know whatcha' mean chile. Help him, Jesus!" Hattie Mae laughed.

Just then Deacon Snow returned with the vacuum. He plugged it in on the wall beside the table with the tithes boxes on top of it. He turned it on while Sister Rose and Hattie Mae were still talking. They shouted for him to turn it off, but he couldn't hear them. Hattie Mae walked up to him to tell him but he couldn't understand what she was saying because of the noise. Hattie Mae walked to the back were the vacuum was plugged in and yanked it out. Sister Rose ran up behind her and stood next to Hattie while she yelled at the old man.

"What the heck you do that fo' ol' woman!"

"Didn't you hear me and Rose in here talking?"

"No! Ya'll don't be talking about anything anyways; all you two do is gossip and talk about people. The Lawd gonna strike you down if you keep that up!"

"I tell you what, I'm a strike you down if you don't turn that devilish thing off!" She tried to get past Rose, but she held her back.

"You hear me, ya ol' coot!"

"Ol' woman take your non-directin' tired behind on over there and finish what y'all was supposed to be doin and leave me alone!"

"Lawd Jesus, keep me near the cross Heavenly Father! Lawd, give me strength not to cut this ol' fish eyed fool!" She pulled out her plastic knife, while the Deacon dropped the vacuum and put up his dukes.

"Y'all two stop this foolishness now, and let's get back to work," Rose said laughing.

~ ~ ~ ~

It was 9 am Monday morning as Rayford sat in the principal's office of Rosa Parks High School waiting patiently to be seen by Principal Victor Gonzales. He had a long night with Van-Helving and her group. He learned earlier that morning that the body in the basement of the fun house was the hot dog vender, Mr.Sams. The other victims' bodies were too decayed to identify them. Only through dental x-rays and files will he find out who those persons were. To occupy his time he reached over the wooden oak table in front of him and grabbed the latest addition of *Time* magazine, thumbing through it. He even managed to read an article that caught his attention.

The sounds of typewriters and phones ringing disturbed him for a moment, then the secretary's rang Mr. Gonzales's phone.

"Mr. Gonzales, there's a detective out here who would like to speak to you." She paused for a minute listening to his reply. "Yes Sir, I'll send him right in." She hung up the phone then got up and approached Rayford.

He watched the beautiful Caucasian woman with blonde hair coming closer. She wore a white shirt with a brown plaid blazer and matching pants. Her hair was neatly done in a French braid. Her stunning blue eyes glowed when she smiled.

"Mr. Gonzales will see you now, Sir. Come this way," she said.

"Thank you." Rayford replaced the magazine, stood up and followed her. She opened the door for him; he went in and closed the door.

~ ~ ~ ~

Victor Gonzales was a good-looking man in his early 40's,

Rayford guessed. His hair was jet black and painstakingly jelled back. He sat at his desk looking over the attendance file for the month of November. Victor wore a mini plaid, long sleeved shirt with a back yoke, a beige tie and beige pocket pants with button flap pockets. Rayford wasn't in the mood for fancy dressing. He decided on his black long sleeve shirt, blue jeans and sneakers. Victor stood up to shake Rayford's forthcoming hand.

"Good morning, Detective. Please, have a seat." Victor said.

Rayford sat down in the chair directly in front of Gonzales. His office had plaques and awards around the room of his greatest achievements while being principal of the school. The large window lay in the back behind Gonzales's office chair. Pictures of his family adorned the huge oak desk along with his phone and other files. A desk lamp sat on the right, while his nameplate sat directly in front of it. Rayford noticed his waste paper basket was full and in need of emptying. The plush brown carpet matched the off beige wall that was in the large room.

"How can I help you on this wonderful day?"

"Well, Mr. Gonzales…"

"Please call me, Victor."

"Ah.. yeah okay. Well, Victor.." He cleared his throat and pulled out his note pad and pen. He sat straddled in the chair. He leaned in with both arms on the desk, and Rayford laid his face on to his left hand and with his right hand he began to write down information. "I'm doing an investigation on the murder of one of you students. Jade Wilson."

"Yes, I've heard. She was a wonderful girl. She will be sorrowfully missed around here. She was an excellent student and she made the honor roll countless times. What a shame to have such an awful situation happen to such a sweet young lady."

"I'm quite sure she will be missed by all who knew her and loved her," Rayford said.

"What I would like to know about is a rumor that has been flying around the school; about one of your teachers, a Mr. Brinkley."

"Paul Brinkley? What rumor has been going around about him

now?"

"Now? So there have been other alleged allegations against him?"

"Well, yes, but that's because most of the kids here don't particularly care for him. He's a very strict man and has his own values and opinions on life, that the kids around here don't take to very well."

"I see. But the rumor that I'm interested in has to do with an incident between Ms. Wilson and Brinkley."

"I have no idea what you're talking about detective."

"Well, let me try to refresh your memory. According to a few of Ms. Wilson's friends and her parents, Mr. Brinkley frequently picked on Ms. Wilson for no apparent reason."

"As I've stated before Detective, Mr. Brinkley is a very strict man, but as far as him picking on her. I have no idea what you're talking about."

"Alright. Well, would it be possible for me to speak to Mr. Brinkley right now so that I may question him?"

"I have no problem with that, besides I would like to know what went on myself, but unfortunately Mr. Brinkley has not shown up for work yet. Another teacher told me that he did attend the senior dance last night, he may have slept late, I don't know."He shrugged his shoulders.

"He hasn't called in yet either. But you're welcome to speak to any of the other teachers here if you like or any of the students."

"Thank you, Sir. I appreciate that. Is it possible that you could get the names of her classmates that I can speak to?"

"Yes, I'll have my secretary get right on it. In the mean time is there anything else I can assist you with?"

"No, the list will do just fine. I will also speak with the teachers."

Gonzales got up, as well as Rayford. They shook hands and said their good byes. Gonzales went to the door and called his attractive secretary in his office. He explained what he needed for her to get. She willingly accepted her responsibility. Rayford walked out with her.

~ ~ ~ ~

74

PSYCHOPATHIC

The corridors of Rosa Parks High were silent; all of the students were in class studying or listening to there teachers about that day's lesson. Rayford walked down to room 304a and knocked. A 17-year-old, blonde haired boy answered the door. The male teacher stood at the black board writing out an algebra problem, and then asked the other teenagers in the room if anyone knew the answer. He stopped when he saw Rayford standing in the doorway.

"Can I help you, Sir?"

"Yes, my name is Detecive Bradley Rayford. May I speak with you in private?"

"OOOOOH," came the class.

Someone yelled, "Mr. Jones is busted! I guess we don't have to study for that test next week ,huh?" Everyone cheered until Mr. Jones turned around and told the class to be quiet. Jones asked one of his better kids to watch over the class and write down anyone's name who misbehaved while he was gone. He led Rayford back out into the hall and closed the door.

"Now, what can I help you with?"

"What is your name, Sir?"

"I'm Mr. Jones. Look, what's this all about. I'm in the middle of teaching a class here."

"I understand that. I'll only be a minute."

Jones leaned against the lockers that were on the left of his room door. Rayford continued.

"Mr. Jones, I'm here doing an investigation of the murder of one of the students here. Her name was…"

"Yeah, I know who you're talking about. Jade Wilson."

"Right. Would you know anything about the rumor that went around about her and another colleague of your's, a Mr. Paul Brinkley?"

"Detective, let me try to explain something to you. You see, Paul Brinkley is a self-righteous son-of-a-bitch and these kids know it. What I found out about Brinkley is that he hates to be corrected and considers himself always right, never wrong. What happened is Jade knew just a little bit more than Brinkley did on a certain subject.

75

Brinkley didn't like it. For some ungodly reason he confronted her about it after class. He threatened to give her a bad grade. Jade was only voicing her opinion and Brinkley felt he was being disrespected by Jade's knowledge of the subject and for saying what she had on her mind that's all it was Detective. I personally feel that Brinkley was way out of line and he should have been suspended without pay, but who am I to put my two cents in all this?"

"So, what you're saying is, the allegations are true and Brinkley did have a vendetta against her?"

"Yes sir. If you asked me if Brinkley thought he could have gotten away with it, he would have turned her over his knee and given her a good spanking."

"I see. Could you possibly direct me towards Brinkley's classroom?"

"Sure. Go down the hall, take the steps up to the third floor, hang a right. His room number is 405. But I don't see what going to his room will do. He's not there."

"Thank you for your time, Mr. Jones."

"No problem. I hope you find the person that did this."

"Yeah, me too."

Mr. Jones went back into the classroom. Rayford noticed before he had finished talking with Brinkly, the class had become rowdy. Rayford followed Mr. Jones's directions. He opened the door to room 405 and went in. The first thing he noticed were pictures of famous leaders in time: Rosa Parks, Abraham Lincoln, George Washington and so forth plastered all around the room. Desks were lined up neatly in a row. To the left of him were bookcases with history books tidily lined up. The chalkboard was behind him while Brinkley's desk was in front of the black board.

Rayford decided to have a look inside Brinkley's desk. He opened the middle center drawer. Nothing but broken off pieces of chalk, paper clips, markers, pens and a few marked test papers. He opened the drawer on the right only to find textbooks and an attendance book. In the drawer to the left were blank test papers, a stapler, and pencils. Rayford's patience was wearing thin. He got up and headed toward the back of the room where a closet was on the left. He opened it and found a sweater of Brinkley's, he assumed. Over top was a shelf with papers and other school supplies, when something caught his eye. In the back was a medium sized black book. He reached for it. It was Brinkley's diary. Rayford began reading it.

April 21ˢᵗ

Today was very nerve wrecking. My students all think they know everything and they don't know shit! Particularly, Ms. Wilson. How dare she defy me in front of everyone! She made me look like a total asshole! We were discussing the war with the Nazis. Hitler, in my eyes, was a great man strategically wise. But noooooo, not to Ms. Wilson! All she talked about was how he was so prejudice against the Jews and other nationalities, and how I should be ashamed of myself for even saying that he was great. Now everybody thinks I'm some kind of prejudice fool! Oh Ms. Wilson I will have my day! You will pay for making me look like an idiot!

Just then Rayford heard the door open, it was Brinkley. He came in and sat his brief case on his desk; he noticed someone was in the back in the closet. Brinkley came from behind him. Rayford slowly turned to face Brinkley. He prayed to God that Brinkley didn't see what he had in his hand. He slowly put the small diary in his front pants pocket out of view from Brinkley.

"Excuse me, would you mind telling me what you're doing snooping around in my closet? And while you're at it, who the hell are you?"

"I'm Detective Rayford." He reached in his pocket and pulled out his badge, then continued, " I'm doing an investigation on the death of your student, Jade Wilson."

"Okay, but that doesn't explain why you were sneaking around in my closet."

"That's true. Mr. Brinkley, I need to ask you some questions."

"Such as?"

"Alright, let me give it to you straight. There have been recent allegations against you concerning mistreatment of Ms. Wilson. By any chance is that true?"

"Yes, that's true. We've had disagreements, but I still don't see what that has to do with you in my closet."

"Don't you get it, Brinkley? Everyone's a suspect in my book until I find out other wise."

"Me? Why? Over a rumor? Granted it is true that we did argue, but that doesn't make me a murderer!"

Rayford thought if he could get the man angry, he would take his mind off of what he was doing in the closet. So far it was working.

"If I'm such a suspect as you called it, why aren't you reading me my rights now, huh? Why didn't you arrest me as soon as I came in the door? You know why you didn't? Because you knew you didn't have anything on me! That's why!" Brinkley said angrily.

"Don't play innocent with me," Rayford said. "I know how you're twisted mind works!"

"Listen Rayford, or what ever the hell your name is, I've had a terrible night and I didn't get any sleep, ok? I don't have time for your shenanigans alright?"

"What do you mean by that?"He turned back to face Brinkley again. Rayford tried to be sympathetic, but he couldn't muster it up. But he did notice when Brinkley came in, he was a little freaked out from something. But from what? He didn't know.

"Do you really want to know the answer to that, Detective?"

"If I didn't ,I wouldn't have asked you. Now would I?"

Brinkley disregarded his sarcastic remark and continued.

"What would you say if I told you I saw the sick bastard you're looking for, hmm? Or better yet, What if I told you I saw him kill again last night?" He looked Rayford in the eyes; fear crept into his face.

"I'd say, tell me what you know."

"Why should I? After the way you just spoke to me?"

Rayford felt a little remorseful for his actions. He took a deep breath.

"Okay, I'm sorry. Now tell me what you know."

"Last night was our school dance for the seniors, I went as a chaperone."

"OK, I'm listening."

"Anyway, I saw a few of my students. I tried to be polite to one of them by asking them to dance, which by the way, she refused."

"Get to the point, Brinkley."

"Alright, as the night went on, I saw a couple of my students leave early so I decided to follow them. You know to check up on them and make sure they didn't get into trouble," he lied.

"Uh, huh continue." But he didn't let on that he already knew he was there.

"I followed them to this abandoned fun house."

"What the hell were they doing out there?"

"I don't know, but I know that I'm sorry I followed them!"

"Some wacko was in there! It was tall and it had a top hat and a clown face!" He gestured his top hat and body length to Rayford. Brinkley's voice started to crack and his eyes broke slightly into tears.

"I saw him kill a student of mine, James Stafford. He died right in front of me!"

"How did he die?"

"Whoever this person was, he had no mercy, no compassion whatsoever for human life! I saw him take a knife to James's head and ram his body into the glass wall that was behind us."

"How did you escape?"

"When he rammed James's body behind me, I fell back under them, then ran. He chased me, I fought for my life, and he had a knife on me. I managed to kick it out of his hand and then punch him in his face. Not too much later I caught up with the kids that were there. It came after us again as we were leaving, but we all got away."

"What are you talk..."

"Wait, there's more," Brinkley said.

"Okay, go on."

"While we were running out of there, I heard Chris scream that her boyfriend was still inside. Not only is his body in there, but a few others as well."

"You're telling me that there are dead bodies out there?"

"Yes. Somebody needs to get out there quick."

"I'm on it. Let me know if you remember anything else about what happened last night. Here's my fax number and card." He threw it on the desk.

The school bell rang. Brinkley looked at his watch. "Listen, Detective, my next class is about to begin."

"Right, I'm out of here. But remember one thing Brinkley."

"What's that?"

He bent down to where Brinkley was sitting in his chair behind the desk. He invaded Brinkley's space by being directly in his face. He grabbed him by the collar.

"I'm watching you. You got that?"

"What for? I told you everything I know!"

"Yeah, I know, but I would advise you not to leave this state. As far as I'm concerned, everyone is a suspect until I get some answers around here! If I so much as catch you squatting down wiping your ass, you'd better tell me it's because you just took a shit! You got me, Brinkley! Or so help me God, if I find out you had anything to do with this case, I'll have your pervert ass thrown in the pen so fast you'll be cryin' for your ma'ma! And trust me, Ma'Ma couldn't help you, and Big Bubba wouldn't mind makin' you his bitch!" Rayford yelled. Rayford's saliva sprayed on Brinkley's face.

He disgustingly used the back of his left hand to wipe it away.

"Get your hands off me!" Brinkley punched at his hands.

Rayford thought about striking him, but decided to let him go. Brinkley fell back in his chair. Rayford got up then turned and walked away.

"You're fuckin' crazy!" Brinkley said, as he tried to collect himself. "What kind of detective are you that goes around scaring the shit out of his victims?" he shouted.

Rayford paused at the door, looked at him over his shoulder.

"The kind that will throw your vindictive ass in the joint if I find out you're lying to me!" He walked out and slammed the door.

Anger took over Brinkley's body. He pounded his fist on the desk and thought. His face twisted with anger. *You think you've got me all figured out detective, but I have news for you! Mr. Self-fuckin-righteous! I know more than what you think I do!*

CHAPTER 7
THE SURPRISE

Rayford awoke to the sound of his radio alarm clock going off on his night stand. He reached over with his right arm and shut it off. He wasn't in the mood to get up, but he knew he had to. He called Skyler's father the previous night to tell him he had to speak with his son one more time. He sat up in his bed and yawned ,then pulled the covers back to get out the bed.

The wooden floor in his bedroom was cold. He turned on his lamp then headed for the bathroom. Rayford opened the sliding door to his shower. He turned it on and got undressed. He stood there for a moment letting the hot water soak into his skin. He dreaded going over to Skyler's to antagonize the boy, but he knew he had to get some answers and he knew the boy hadn't told him the whole truth the first time they met. *Why didn't he tell his father or anybody else for that matter about Jade's pregnancy?* he thought.

Rayford had already questioned all of Jade's classmates in school and all of them told him what he already knew. *Could it be that he was ashamed to tell his father and he knew his dad would be totally upset with him if he found out? Or could it be that he thought his father would do serious bodily harm to him?* Either way, Rayford thought he knew that's how he would have reacted to the news. Well, maybe not doing a number on him, but he would certainly be highly upset with his only son.

Rayford grabbed the soap off of the shower rack and lathered up. He rinsed off and opened the sliding door for his towel. He was about to dry off his back, when he heard a knock at the door. He took the towel and wrapped it around him then headed for the front door.

"Who is it?" Rayford answered.

"It's Sharie, Mr. Rayford. I need to speak with you."

"Sure. Just hold a sec, okay?"

Rayford didn't wait for a reply as he hurried back into the bedroom to find something to put on. He pulled out his blue Old Navy sweatshirt and jeans. He looked like a bunny jumping around trying to hurry up and put his pants on. Rayford ran around tiding up the place before he opened the door for her.

"Did I catch you at a bad time?"

"Sort of. I just got out of the shower."She could see he was out of breath from all the running around he was doing.

"Oh, I'm sorry. I'll come back when it's more convenient for you. I should have called before I came anyway."

"Oh no, it's no problem. Come in and have a seat. I was about to make myself some coffee anyway. Would you like some?" He walked towards the kitchen.

"No, it's alright. Coffee gives me heartburn," she yelled into the kitchen after him as she sat down. "You've got a nice place here."

"Thanks. I try to keep it as neat as I can."

Sharie knew he was lying because on the couch in between the pillows she noticed a pair of his underwear tucked in between them. Even though he lied about his house cleaning abilities. she did notice that his place fit for his personality. She liked the beige reclining love seat that she was sitting on. The matching couch was on the opposite side of it. There was a round glass coffee table in the middle and a beige throw rug under it. To the right of her were the fireplace and a mini bar. Directly in front was the thirty six-inch flatscreen television, which hung on the white wall.

Rayford was a football-type of guy and the evidence showed with an autographed Donovan Mcnabb Eagle's jersey encased on the wall to the left of where she was sitting. Football memorabilia could be seen around the large room.

The smell of Rayford's coffee began to fill the room. The aroma brought her mind back to what she came there for. Rayford came back out and sat on the couch. He put his coffee mug down on the table.

"Now what's on your mind?"

"I came to confess something to you that I didn't tell you earlier at the police station."

"Really? I'm all ears."

Sharie fidgeted in the chair. She didn't feel comfortable about telling him what she had to say. Yet, she knew she had to go through with it. "A few days before Jade was murdered she confided in me about something."

"Go on," Rayford coaxed her.

"She came to me crying and very upset," she said, with her arm supporting her head as she leaned on the arm of the love seat. "She told me something that could get somebody in a lot of trouble if it ever got out."

"Okay, so what did she tell you?"

"She said she had just came back from the doctor's office and she found out that she was almost two months pregnant."

"Yeah, I know about that."

"You do? How?"

"It's part of my job to find out things about my cases, young lady. So, did Skyler know about this?"

"No, and he still doesn't know."

"Well then. Who would be in trouble then?"

"Mr. Rayford, Jade didn't get pregnant by Skyler. She was pregnant by Mr. Brinkley."

"You're kidding me, right?"

"No, Sir. I'm dead serious."

"You know this could be the end of Brinkley's career right? That's if this is all true; that she was pregnant by him. And that also makes him a prime suspect in this case."

"How?"

"Because, for one thing sweetie, he didn't tell me about the pregnancy and two he had sex with a student. But that's not all. I found his diary in his closet with some incriminating evidence as well."

"Could I ask what was in it?" Sharie was curious.

"I can't reveal that to you, sweetheart, but all I can say is it doesn't look good for Mr. Paul Brinkley."

Jasmine walked out of the 7-11 with her bag of groceries towards her black 2003 Maxima Ultra. Nicole, Sharie, and Nadine had gone out to the movies in Nicole's father's car. Jasmine wished she had gone with them, but she had promised to help her mom out around the house the night before.

The street lamps illuminated the tops of the cars and pavement. It was 12 am and the street was practically empty, except for a few stray cars traveling up and down the street. A few couples strolled along in the night air. One couple walked with their arms around each other, huddling close to block out the cold. Sleet began to come down in tiny flakes of beautiful white crystal shapes. Jasmine didn't like going out so late; being in the streets this time of the night made her feel uneasy.

She wanted to be home cuddled up in front of the television or with a good novel wearing her fluffy gray elephant slippers sipping a cup of hot cocoa. She made it to her car, which was parked in a dark area. When she first arrived, the street lamp was still on, but someone mysteriously broke the light that hung over her car. A piece of broken glass lay on the hood; it shimmered from the light of the moon. She picked it up and examined it. She thought it to be odd, but quickly figured it out when she glanced up and saw what had happened. *Some idiot did this. They should be happy no one was around when they did it,* she thought.

Jasmine put the groceries on the hood while she fumbled in her pocketbook in the dark for her keys. She kept trying to remind herself to clean out the junk in it, but she never got around to it. She did, however, manage to keep her credit cards and ID's in her red wallet. After serious searching, she found the keys and unlocked the door. Jasmine put the groceries on the passenger side and got in. She reached to put the keys in the ignition and drove off into the moonlit night. She bent down and turned the radio on. Her mother had been in the car earlier that day and left WKYW news station on. The report came on about James's death, along with the other 2 people in the fun house. She quickly turned to her station. *I don't need to be reminded of the story again*, she thought. The girl group, Tatu, came on. The melodic sounds of *"All The Things She Said "* filled the car. She turned it up and began singing. Even though she didn't feel safe outside late at night, she felt she would be safe in her car, decidedly taking the long way home. She turned off Ogantz Ave on to Washington Lane. Her song went off, but she left the radio turned up.

The sleet continued to fall like little pieces of glass against her windshield. Jasmine barely noticed the streetlights becoming dimmer as she continued on towards Chew Ave. With the music still blaring, she made a left turn off Washington Lane and down Chew. She came to a traffic light. It was red. She brought her car to a complete stop. A blue '98 Buick pulled up behind her with two teenagers in it.

The male driver argued with his girlfriend. Jasmine watched them from her rear view mirror. The male slapped his girlfriend, while the female cried out from the pain from the swift hand connecting to her face. "What a jerk!" she yelled at the mirror. The light changed. She pressed on the gas and continued driving.

The sound of the car wheels screeching from behind her startled Jasmine. She looked out the rear view mirror and watched the Buick speed around her. She was about to turn away, when out of nowhere she saw the hideous clown face appear in her mirror. She screamed as the intruder grabbed her long black hair and pulled it back until her head banged against the headrest. Her hands lost control of the steering wheel. She felt something synthetic clutch her around her neck from behind. She screamed louder and tried to remove what was strangling her, but she couldn't. Her foot pressed harder on the gas and the car went speeding down the street uncontrollably. Jasmine's legs began to kick and stomp with fury, while her hands continued to try to remove the stocking that was chocking her. But the unmerciful grip of her attacker would not let her go. She reached with one hand frantically to gain control of the car, while her other hand continued to pull at the stocking. All of her attempts were useless. Air started to become scarce as she tried to breathe. The car swerved toward an intersection.

Nicole had just dropped off Nadine and Sharie. She was on her way home when she saw Jasmine's car cut in front of her. She tried to put on the breaks as she banged her hand down on her horn and slammed on the breaks. The long loud sound of a car horn was the last thing Jasmine heard. The car came through and hit the driver's side forcing her to hit a nearby telephone pole. The killer inside the car let her go, and the force of the crash sent its body flying out the back door.

The murderer landed on the sidewalk and rolled a few feet away from the horrifying crash. Amazingly, the assassin got up and ran limping away with only minor injuries. Jasmine's eyes were wide open as her lifeless body slumped against the steering wheel, blood oozed down her face. Sounds of an ambulance and police cars where in the distance, but it was too late for both drivers. Way too late...

~ ~ ~ ~

Chris couldn't sleep as she lay in bed watching the late show. *The Howling: Part One* had just come on. She couldn't understand why she was watching something like this with all the horror she saw in the past few days, but somehow she felt safe in her room watching it. She kept the door cracked with her night-light on the floor under her desk on. Chris sat up in bed and propped her pillows behind her. She sat back in a way that flipped her hair up, letting out a sigh of boredom She grabbed her remote on the night stand and flipped through the channels.

After a few minutes she gave up trying to find anything worth while to watch and called for her toy poodle, Jacks. Chris named him Jacks because it was short for Michael Jackson, her favorite singer's last name. She remembered the first day she saw Jacks. She and Sharie were coming home from school. As they were getting off of the bus, they saw some children mistreating the dog and chasing him. She and Sharie chased the kids away and picked up the dog and took it to her house. She remembered the look on Jacks face; he was lost, cold and scared. He had an expression of *thank you Jesus; someone is here to help me* on his face. They found tags on him and her mother called the S.P.C.A. shelter. They gave her the number to the owners, but there was a mix up with the name of the people that owned him. Jacks didn't belong to them he belonged to Mrs. Hicks her neighbor. She took the dog back to her. She told Chris that he must have broken his chain and got loose, but she also asked Chris if she would be willing to keep him, because she was no longer able to care for him. Chris told her that she would have to ask her mother. She did, and her mother agreed to take him in.

Chris called for him again she thought he might be under her bed. She bent over and looked. He wasn't there. She got up and went to her door and called again. Still nothing. She went back and put on her slippers and robe then crept downstairs. She thought maybe her mother put him in his doghouse out in the enclosed porch behind the kitchen. Her instincts told her something was wrong before she reached the door to the porch. The door had a glass pane in it, and as soon as anyone came to it, his doghouse could be seen sitting in the back in the corner next to the backyard door. Normally, if he were in the doghouse, she could see his face sticking out, but not this time. Chris opened the door and looked around.

She looked in the doghouse. Fear ran through her body like a bolt of lightening, when she turned and saw the back window was open and the screen was busted out. Her mother often left the window open whenever she was back there doing laundry. Her mom had put her old kitchen chair by the window, that's where she often sat while the dryer was running. After examining what had happened Chris ran back through the house and called for her mother. "Mom!" She ran up the stairs. "Mom!"

Her mother opened the door with her face covered in Oil of Olay night cream and her hair in curlers, with her pink robe on. "What's the matter, baby? And why are you up so late?"

"I couldn't sleep mom, Jacks is gone! I can't find him anywhere!"

"What do you mean he's gone?"

"The back window was open Mom. He must have climbed in the chair by the window and jumped out!" Tears started to roll down her cheeks.

"Oh my God! I forgot to close the window when I was out there this afternoon." she said looking at her daughter, who was sitting on the steps, her arms folded and her head down sobbing. "Calm down baby, let's get our clothes on and we'll go and look for him alright?"

"Okay. " Chris said. She slowly got up and went up the steps to her room to change...

~ ~ ~ ~

Captain Jennings stood by his squad car with the door open, leaning on the hood. He was on his car radio talking to the dispatcher. "Get Rayford on the phone! Tell him to get his ass down here pronto!"

"That's a ten four, Sir." the female dispatcher replied.

He bent down inside the car and hung up the mic. Flashing red and blue lights from the top of the police cars encircled the area of the accidental crash. Traffic was being directed around the scene by a cop standing in the middle of the street. Local news crews were there covering the story. Firemen had to use the Jaws of Life to remove the dead bodies from the vehicles. Broken glass lay upon the ground as if someone sprinkled it all over.

Captain Jennings and other officers from the precinct stood around in a circle in their blue uniforms discussing what must have happened.

"It looked like one car came from that directio," one officer said, then he continued. "The other car was speeding uncontrollably down this way. The skid marks stop over by there by the pole."

"Were there any witnesses?" Jennings asked.

"No, people around here are too afraid of the drug dealers and other hoodlums that usually hang out around here this time of night."

"Yeah, it figures."

"Well, did anybody find anything inside the car that was speeding?"

"Yeah, some groceries were in the front all over the passengers side, kinda strange though, we found something else."

"What?"

"Well, in the back seat there was a pair of stockings on the floor. Wanna know what else was strange?"

"Enlighten me," Jennings said, with his index finger and thumb under his chin, listening attentively.

"Someone was in the back seat of the car that crashed into the pole over there."

"How's that?"

"Because, the back door was forced open like somebody forced it open or flew out of it."

"Hmm interesting."

"Did anybody get any info on the licenses plates? And the identity of the drivers?"

"Yep, sure did Captain. The car that hit the pole was registered under a Mr. Jerry Thurman. The deceased driver in the car is his daughter, Ms. Jasmine Thurman, age 18." He paused.

"And the other car?"

"The other accident victim's car is registered under a Mrs. Lavonne Speech and the driver is her daughter, 18-year-old Nicole…" He was about to say something else, when all of the officers and Captain Jennings turned and saw two women running up the street towards them. One of the women was carrying a brown toy poodle.

It was Chris and her mom. Chris put Jacks down. She paused for a moment to take in the horrible scene. Chris could see the paramedics taking the white sheet covered bodies of Jasmine and Nicole and putting them into separate ambulances. Her every instinct told her that it was her friends who were in those cars. Chris and her mother continued running toward the group of men.

"Excuse me!" her mother and Chris said out of breath and crying.

"What's wrong young lady? "Jennings said. He took hold of Chris and pulled her chin up to look in her face.

"Could you tell me what happened?"

"I'm sorry young lady ,but both women were killed in that car crash over there."

"Could you tell me who where in the cars?"

Jennings looked at Chris's mom for reassurance. She nodded.

"Please I need to know!" Chris screamed.

"Jasmine Thurman and Nicole Speech."

"Oh God, when is it going to end?" Chris yelled and cried and almost fell to the ground while holding on to Jennings. Her mother picked her up and held her daughter in her arms. She turned to look at Jennings. "How did this happen?"

"Well ma'am, from what we've come up with, it seems that Ms. Thurman was strangled in the car before Ms. Speech crashed into her."

",So that means somebody was in the car with Jasmine right?" Chris asked.

"It looks that way, ma'am."

Chris broke away from her mother's comforting arms and looked at Jennings. "Jesus! When are you guys going to figure out whose killing all my fucking friends?" Chris yelled and pounded on Jennings chest out of anger.

Jennings tried to hold her, but Chris pushed him away. Her mother restrained her from behind and then turned her around to hug her. Jennings brushed himself off. Just then Rayford pulled up and got out of his car. Jennings face turned red with anger as he watched Rayford walk around his car towards him. He turned back to the two women. "Ma'am I'm going to have to ask you to leave now and let us continue with our investigation."

"We understand, Sir, please forgive my daughter for her outburst. She and her friends have been under a lot of strain since this all began."

"No problem, ma'am. Just take her home and let her rest."

Rayford was standing in front of him while he watched over his shoulder at the two women walking arm and arm back down the street. He waited until they were a few feet away before he dug into Rayford. "Where the hell have you been, Detective?"

"I…" Rayford didn't get to finish.

"Never mind! I don't want to hear anymore of your sorry excuses! You know what? If you don't find out who the fuck is doing all of this shit, I promise you I will have your badge so damn fast it will make your head spin! You got that?" Jennings tone was less than civil.

Rayford was becoming angered by Jennings accusations. He hated to be chastised by Jennings in front of his peers. He wanted so badly to punch his lights out. He knew if he did hit a superior that he would no longer be employed.

Jennings continued. "You've got twenty-four hours, Detective. I want this psycho bastard behind bars, or you will regret it!"

CHAPTER 8
THE TRUTH UNFOLDS

The gymnasium of Rosa Parks High was huge. It had a two-way entrance. One entrance stood in front the other in the back. The white walls were plastered with "Go Cougars!" signs and other posters of encouragement for their basketball team.

The bleachers in the back sat stacked up, except for a few for the students to sit on during gym class. Three retractable walls on the side could open to make the gym smaller. Wooden floors stretched all the way to the back. The basketball courts could be seen on the left and the right of the room. Multicolor mats lay in the back in front of the bleachers. That's where Sharie Nadine, and Chris sat talking about the accidental death of their friends.

"I'm telling you it wasn't an accident!" screamed Chris. "I was there. I saw their bodies! And the captain that was there with us told my Mom and I that Jasmine was strangled before she died."

"Man I can't believe this crap! Nicole was just with us last night! She just dropped us off. Hell, that could have been us in that car! What the hell was she doing going home that way? She only lived a few blocks away from us. Why didn't she just go the normal way, like she always does?" asked Nadine.

"Who knows, Nadine?" Sharie commented. "But it could have been one of us. Let's just say we were lucky. Thank God."

"I want to know why this person is going around killing us off. What did we do to him or her or it? Jasmine was my friend, man. She could be such a noodle sometimes, but I liked her a lot," said Nadine.

"I know what you mean, girl, " Chris said. "Nicole was cool with me. She was the first person I met when I came to this school. I remember how she and I got lost trying to find Brinkley's class on the first day." Chris sat with her head down, scratching her head as if she could come up with an explanation to what had happened.

"Yeah, well, check this out. I got the low down about something," Sharie commented.

"Oh? What?" asked Nadine.

Before she could answer Skyler, Matt and Mark entered from the side door bouncing and throwing a basketball around. They saw the girls sitting on the bleachers and walked over to them.

"Hey, you girls up for a game?" Mark said juggling the ball in his hand.

"Apparently you assholes have no idea as to what happened. Am I right about it?" Nadine started.

"What are you talking about Nadine? And you know what, I'm getting really tired of your smart mouth too!"

"Not that I give a shit about what you think of me and my mouth, but to enlighten you. Jas and Nicole are gone."

"What?" said Mark, Matt and Skyler.

"What are you talking about they're gone?" said Skyler.

"Just what I said! They're dead," Nadine paused and looked down, then back up at Skyler. "They died in a car crash last night Sky."

"Jesus, man!" Skyler yelled ,while the other guys just shook their heads in disbelief.

"Wanna know the messed up part about it?" Nadine said.

"What?"

"Chris said that Jas was killed before she crashed in her car. In other words, somebody was in the car with her."

"Okay I'm tired of this shit!" Mark interjected. "I say we really crack down and try to find out who this person is."

"That's what Chris, Sharie and I've been trying to do, but with not much luck," Nadine said.

"Well, I did go and see Detective Rayford last night at his apartment, and he gave me some info that I think could help us out," Sharie started.

"Oh and what's that?" said Chris.

"Well, I wasn't going to tell you guys about it because Jade swore me to secrecy, but I think it's time you all know. Before Jade was killed she confided in me about something that I'm sure she hadn't told anybody. Not even you, Sky."

"Spit it out, Sharie!" Nadine cried with curiosity.

"Okay."Sharie took a deep breath, "Jade told me that she was two months pregnant a few days before she was killed."

Skyler almost fell on the floor at the news. "What? Why didn't she tell me? Oh, my God!"

"Sky, she didn't tell you because..." Sharie took another deep breath.

"Because what!"

"Because the baby wasn't your's, Sky."

"WHAT! Oh shit, the bitch played me? You're telling me she played me? Is that what you're saying, Sharie?"

"Yeah, but you could be a little respectful Sky, after all she is dead! Calling her out of her name won't change what's happened."

"You're right. I'm sorry, I take that back." Tears came to his eyes as he lashed out punching at the air as if Brinkley was standing there.

"I'm sorry, Sky." Sharie stood up and hugged him.

"I have something else to tell you that's just as bad, but I didn't tell Rayford."

"Wait, first tell me who's the father?"

Sharie pulled away from him, and looked him in the eye, "Sky, I'd rather not say."

"Sharie, I have a right to know."

She looked at him sobbing, not wanting to say anymore, but she couldn't avoid it. She had to tell him. "It was Brinkley; he raped her." Everyone gasped.

"Sharie, why didn't you tell Rayford she was raped? What are trying to do, protect Brinkley?" asked Nadine.

"Hell no! I was just scared!"

"Scared of what? Telling the truth and putting his nasty behind in the nut house where he belongs? Come on, Sharie, you have to call Rayford and tell him what you told us."

Sharie stood there holding Skyler and looking at Nadine with tears in her eyes. She knew she was right. She reached in her pocket for her cell phone, but Skyler's sudden movement and outburst made her drop it out of her hands.

"Jesus! I'm going to kill him!" he yelled pulling away from Sharie angrily, then ran for the doors. Sharie and the rest of the gang ran after him and caught him by the arm. Sharie reached him first.

"Sky, listen to me! Killing him won't solve anything. All we can do is let the police handle this."

"What kind of teacher is he, Sharie? Huh? Doesn't he know he could go to jail for this? Better yet, get fired from teaching period?"

Matt jumped in. "Look, I'm sure he knows all that, and I understand how you're feeling right now, but like Sharie said, man, killing him won't solve anythin," said Matt.

"So what do we do now?" said Skyler.

"We calm down and go upstairs to Brinkley's class and act normal. I'm going to call Rayford now and tell him everything. Once I do then I'm sure Rayford will be here soon to arrest his 'robbing the cradle ass!' Now, are you cool?" said Sharie.

"Yeah, I'm cool."

"Alright you guys, go ahead and I'll meet you in the class room." Sharie said pulling out her cell phone and dialing Rayford.

~ ~ ~ ~

Upstairs in Brinkley's classroom students sat on top of desks and in their chairs conversing with one another. A few were rowdy and some even threw paper and things around. One person was bold enough to plug up his CD player and turn on the radio. Chris, Nadine, Matt, and Skyler were scattered in different spots around the room. Skyler went to the back of the room to grab a history book, having left his at home. Nadine was one of the rowdy ones yelling at somebody in the middle of the classroom. She sat down quickly when she saw Brinkley standing in the doorway. Brinkley could not believe the chaotic scene that was before him. His face became red with anger. Sharie came in behind him and sat down in her seat in front of him and got out her notebook and pen and began writing a note to Chris. Before she could finish, Brinkley snatched it off of her desk and crumbled it.

"Excuse me!" Brinkley yelled. Everyone turned around and looked at him, ignored him and went back to doing what they were doing before he came in.

"I SAID EXCUSE ME!" Brinkley boomed. This time everyone sat down in their seats and faced him. "Has everyone gone crazy around here? You kids know better!"

Skyler spoke up. "Maybe if you didn't go around being such a sleaze ball, everybody would have more respect for you!"

Brinkley walked up to Skyler's desk and leaned on it with his right hand. He bent down and pointed his finger at him. Skyler had nothing but contempt in his eyes. He wanted so badly to punch him in his mouth, but he didn't move.

"Now, you listen to me you little punk! I don't know what you're talking about, but I guarantee you I will find out and I will get back to you. In the mean time, you just sit there and shut your little grubby mouth!" Brinkley's back was turned away from Sharie and she quickly wrote out the note and handed it to Chris who was sitting next to her. It read:

I called Rayford and told him everything.
He should be here in a few minutes.
Pass this on to the rest of our crew.

She handed it to Chris. She read it and passed it on. Brinkley came back to the front of the class. He slammed his brief case on his desk, which caught everyone by surprise.

"Now that I have your undivided attention let's begin where we left off with the civil war. Now, everyone open your books to page thirty-eight."It was almost in unison as the sound of the books being opened and slammed on the desks filled the room. Brinkley picked up a piece of chalk from in front of the chalkboard and started writing. He turned back around to face the class and folded his arms in front of him, with a smirk on his face.

"Incidentally, there will be a test on this, next Friday." Moans and groans came from all over the room. "So I hope you people have been studying. If not I suggest you do so starting this week."

Chris leaned over to Sharie and whispered, "Little does he know his nerdy ass will be making license plates by next week, and he won't be wearing that simple ass smirk on his face either!"

Brinkley looked up and noticed Chris whispering to Sharie. "Ms. Jones, do you have something you would like to share with the rest of the class? You know it's quite rude to whisper in front of someone."

"Well, Mr. Brinkley, if you weren't being so nosey, you wouldn't have seen me whispering in the first place, now would you?" The sound of laughter went across the room like the wind.

"Quiet! You kids are so…" Before he could finish his sentence a message came on the school's P.A. system. *"Mr. Brinkley, please report to the main office."* Brinkley's face had the look of curiosity on it as he went to the school phone by the door and called for a replacement to watch over the class.

A few moments later Chris'a favorite teacher, Mr. Jamison, walked into the room. It took everything in her to not stare at the gorgeous man that came in. Sharie couldn't help but smile and make googly eyes at him. She turned and looked at Nadine, who was too busy snickering at Chris. Brinkley picked up his brief case and keys off of his desk. He never left his stuff behind; he was always too afraid that somebody would try to steal from him. He left out and headed down the hall towards the office.

~ ~ ~ ~

Rayford sat in the principal's office at the desk trying to explain why he had come back to the school. Rayford had brought another officer with him, who was in uniform. Principal Gonzales was adamant about arresting Brinkley in his classroom in front of his students. Not that anyone cared about what happened to the teacher, it was the significance of it all. It took every ounce of Rayford's being to not go and arrest Brinkley himself. He hated scum like him, especially the ones that go around raping under-aged females. He hated any man who raped women. He loved all people, but women had a special place in his heart. Rayford thought of them as delicate flowers who needed to be treated with respect and love. His only downfall was that he couldn't keep his own wife happy.

Always out in the street risking his life for other people, drove her crazy. She often told him how she felt neglected ,and when he was home he would always be too tired. He never meant to treat her that way, but he couldn't help it. His job was way too demanding. He was in the middle of telling Gonzales who it was that was accusing Brinkley of the rape charges, when Brinkley came in the room. Brinkley knew something was up when he saw Rayford and the officer in the room.

Rayford came right to the point. "Mr. Brinkley, I'm sorry, but I'm going to have to place you under arrest for the rape of Ms. Jade Wilson, and for suspicion of murder."

"Murder? Rape? What are you talking about! I didn't rape anyone!" The officer standing behind him put the handcuffs on him as he tried resisting arrest.

"Brinkley, we have a witness that says you raped Ms. Wilson, and we also know Ms. Wilson was two months pregnant with your child before she was killed!" Rayford yelled.

Brinkley continued to protest. "I'm telling you I didn't do anything!" He tried to squirm and pull away from the officer who was holding him, but the officer had too good of a grip on his arm.

"Brinkley, just go with them. If you're innocent of the charges, it will be proven in court. But, as of this day you're suspended indefinitely!" Gonzales said.

"Jesus! I'm telling you I'm innocent of this, Mr. Gonzales! You've got to believe me!" said Brinkley. Tears of mercy began to swell in his eyes.

Rayford invaded Brinkley's space and grabbed him by the collar, almost knocking over the desk lamp on Gonzales's desk trying to get to Brinkley. "Just save the bull crap Brinkley! I told you if I found out you had anything to do with this case, that I'd be back! You scum bag, piece of shit!" He let him go. "Take him outta here! His presence is making me sick to my stomach!"

The officer started toward the door with Brinkley in tow. Brinkley continued to proclaim his innocence while being pulled out the door. "I didn't do anything, you've got the wrong man I tell you!"

CHAPTER 9
THE ERADICATOR

Dr. Judith Van-Helving sat near her window length wise on her couch, with her leg propped up, reading a romance novel. Her eyes were red and getting tired ,so she removed her glasses off of her face. She could feel a migraine coming on. She closed the book and stared out the window. Memories of her daughter flooded her mind. She continued staring and daydreaming.

She saw her daughter playing around the tire swing under the big oak tree in her front yard. She remembered how she loved that swing and how she loved to have Judith push her on it. Her daughter's squeals of joy and laughter brought tears of joy to her eyes. It seemed to her like only yesterday that she was in that yard playing hide and go seek and other children's games with her only child.

Sarah was only thirteen years old when she passed away from AIDS related complications during an accident. She contracted the disease from a blood transfusion seven years prior. Her, Sarah, and her husband, Mitch, were in a car crash coming home from the movies one Saturday night. Mitch, who was driving at the time, died on the scene. Sarah was rushed to the hospital clinging to life. Judith, on the other hand, was lucky that she came out with only minor injuries. Some how Sarah removed her safety belt and almost flew threw the windshield. The force from her hitting her head on the front seat broke her neck. She had lost a lot of blood from the wound she received from the windshield glass cutting her around her neck and face.

Judith began to cry uncontrollably. She got up from the couch and reached for her crutches that were lying next to her. She hobbled through the living room and dining room to the basement door in the kitchen. Turning on the light she took the steps one by one down to the bottom. She limped to the back where a hidden panel door stood and she pushed it open. She went further underground. Judith had this room specifically built a few years after Sarah died. Originally, it was supposed to be her study room, but she had other plans for it once it was finished.

She turned on the light and reached in the closet next to it and pulled out her black coat with one button missing. Blood spot stains from her previous victims were splattered meticulously over the front of it. She tried everything to get those stains out to no avail. Judith stood for a moment and examined the coat again. At one point she took luminol spray and examined it under a blue flourescent light that she stole from her lab at the hospital. She even tried household products to try to remove it, but the bloodstains still showed up.

Judith reached over the top shelf and found her hunting knife. She looked at it and laughed horrifically at the thought of where the knife plunged into her frightened sufferers. She kept the old knife she used on her first victim as some sort of trophy of her accomplishment. She became angry with herself for leaving it at the crime scene of Jade Wilson, but was happy when Rayford brought it back to the lab the night Jade was killed. Judith sat her crutches against the wall and put on her robe. She put the knife back and moved her hand around the top shelf searching for her box of plastic gloves. She put a pair in her pocket.

Judith turned and looked around the room. She was impressed at the sight. The room was filled with scientific equipment, a huge computer aligned the left side of the wall on the right. Two hyperbolical tubes filled with hydraulic solution stood in back of her metal lab table. The sounds of bubbling noises from the cylinders filled the room. Flourescent lights beamed from the bottom of each tube as the sounds of computer noises and flashing lights played in the background. Another door stood on the wall to the left with a large see through picture window. This was Judith's control room. She walked over to it and opened the door turning on the switch. Inside was another computer board, except it laid in front of her like a switchboard in a recording studio. She sat in her chair at the desk and turned it on. Lights lit up the panel while she sat and toyed with other controls. She pressed one button, which simply read: *Arise!*

Slowly and gradually the dead body of her daughter's cryogenic body appeared inside the chamber directly in front of her. Previously inserted blood filled hoses that lead from her neck down floated around her. All the years of scientific study paid off for Judith. She had preserved her daughter's body for so many years while she searched for the perfect blood type. B negative. *It took a lot of work to find it, honey, but Mommy did it and soon you will live again*, she thought.

~ ~ ~ ~

Everyone in Brinkley's class stood staring out the window, watching Brinkley being escorted into a squad car. Brinkley paused and looked up at the cheering class and gave them a wicked smile. Rayford pushed Brinkley's head down so he could get inside the back seat. He looked up to see what Brinkley was smiling about. He shooed the class to go back to their seats away from the window. Everyone walked back to his or her appropriate seats.

"What did Brinkley do?" asked one red headed female classmate.

Nadine spoke up. "Isn't it bad enough that he was creep? Regardless to what he did, but since you asked he did something to Jade before she passed. Something really bad."

"Well, I gathered that much!' the red head said sarcastically.

"Look girl, it's best that you don't know what happened, okay. You knew how Brinkley was, so let it go at that. And you better watch that tone because I'm not the one, okay?"

"Is that a threat?"

"Nope, that's a promise! So I suggest you take your little bony ass on back to your seat before you regret it!"

"Whatever!" the red head said, while rolling her eyes.

"Yeah I know, whatever!" Nadine rolled her eyes back at her and sat next to Chris.

"Don't you ever quit?" asked Chris.

"She got smart with me. I didn't do anything to her!"

"Whatever, Nadine," Chris chuckled.

Nadine started copying off of the black board then put her pen down and turned to Chris."Hey, why don't we go up to the hospital after school and have some fun online?"

"Okay, I've got some research to do anyway."

"Girl, I'm not going up there to do any work! I want to check out some hotties!" she laughed.

"You're crazy, girl!"

"Yeah I know, but you love me!"

"True," Chris laughed. They were still laughing when the substitute teacher turned away from the board and chastised them. Just as he was about to say something else to them, Rayford came back in. He approached the teacher. "I need to speak to Sharie for a moment."

"Okay."He called for Sharie, who sat behind Skyler. Skyler heard everything Rayford said to the teacher.

"Why does he want to see you?" Skyler asked, as Sharie got up to go to the front of the class. She turned back to face him.

"I don't know."Sharie walked outside the class with Rayford in toe. He closed the door behind him and spoke to her in the hallway.

"Listen, I'm going to need you to testify against Brinkley in court. Can you do that for me?"

"Yeah, sure. I would love to see that scum bag get exactly what he deserves!"

"That's my girl! Oh, and by the way, I want to know if you could do something else for me."

"Anything."

He reached inside his pocket and pulled out an envelope. "I need for you to take this to Dr. Van-Helving for me. It's very important and I need her expert opinion on it."

"Sure, no problem. I'll take it over there after school."

"No sweetheart, I need you to do this now. I've already got permission from your parents to get you out of school early."

"Cool, let me get my stuff. Oh, and I need her address."

"I got it right here." He pulled out the address from his other pants pocket and handed it to her. "I need to go back to the station and finish the booking process on Brinkley. I'll call you later to make sure you got home alright."

"Alright." Sharie tucked the envelope inside her jean pocket and went back inside. Skyler, Chris, Nadine, Matt and Mark watched as she came back in and grabbed her things. They all wondered what was going on. Only Skyler, who whispered to her, could ask. Sharie bent down to hear him. "Where are you off too?"

"Detective Rayford needs me to go over to Van-Helvings' to drop something off for him," she whispered back.

"Who's Van-Helving?"

"She works down at the morgue at the hospital. I think she's the one that did the autopsy report on Jade and James."

"See what you can find out. If anybody knows anything it would be her and Rayford."

"I will Sky, I promise."Sharie patted his back and grabbed her things and left.

~ ~ ~ ~

The police station was busy as ever. Captain Jennings yelled and screamed as usual at another officer working on another cases. The door to the captain's office was open and everyone in the station could hear him bad-mouthing the rookie policeman. He finally slammed the door and continued screaming and acting like a buffoon.

Rayford sat at his desk shaking his head in disbelief of the captain's actions. He decided to give Jake a call since he already knew Van-Helving took the day off. After going through the formalities with the receptionist, he got Jake on the line.

"Hey! Rayford, my favorite person!"

"Cut with the bull shit, man! I want to know if you found out anything since the last time we talked."

"Well, what do you know? The king of assholes wants my help!"

"Look, Jake, I don't have time for this, okay? Just tell me if you know anything."

"Hmm, let me see, well, whoever this person is that's doing all of the killings is very particular about their victims."

"What do you mean by that?"

"It seems that your killer likes only people with B positive blood."

"I already know about that. Van-Helving told me about it a few days ago. But how did you manage to find out about it?"

"You know, I do have a brain, which is something you lack."

"Did I ever tell you about the dreams I've been having about you eating my lasagna and keeling over at my dinner table?"

"No, but I'm sure if it were your wife's' recipe…" Rayford hung up the phone.

~ ~ ~ ~

The sixth floor of Benjamin Bannaker Hospital was quiet. Some patients had gone downstairs for x-rays, while others lay in bed watching different TV shows. The R.N., Mrs. Johnson, who was on duty, had gone to the cafeteria to get coffee. She left a nurse in charge until she came back, but she was busy taking care of a patient down the hall.

Nadine peeked around the nurses's station to see if anyone was around. She caught a glimpse of a nurse going into a patient's room. She and Chris hid behind the wall to the nurse's station.

"Come on nobody's here,"she said.

Chris protested for a moment. "I don't know about this, Nadine. Maybe we should wait until Mrs. Johnson comes back."

"And then what? Have her tell us to get out? You know she wouldn't let us get online and fool around when she's here."

"Yeah, but we could get into trouble you know."

"Just leave it to me. No one's going to do anything."

"I hope you're right."

"You know what? I've changed my mind about looking for guys I've got a better idea," Nadine said as they walked to the computer in front of them. Chris sat down in front of it, while Nadine stood behind her.

"What now?"

"Why don't we do something really interesting?"

"Like what?"

PSYCHOPATHIC

"Are you up to doing some hacking?"

"What are you talking about, Nadine?"

"You know what I'm talking about. You're the only one that knows how to do it."

"Shit, come on Nadine! Why do you always have to be the one to get us into major trouble all the time?"

"Because it wouldn't be me if I didn't." Nadine poked Chris's head from behind. "Come on it will be fun!"

Chris sighed and shook her head. "Okay, what are we trying to get into? The federal government? What?"

"No, stupid! I was thinking along the lines of maybe... hospital records."

"Hospital records? Oh, now I know you've lost your mind!"

"Just do it, Chris, before that nurse comes back."

"You do realize that if I get caught, you will be sharing the blame with me right?"

"Yeah I know, now get on with it. Go to records," Nadine said.

"No, duh?" Chris said sarcastically. She clicked records, but a security warning came up.

"*Authorized Personal Only,*" the screen flashed.

"Damn!" Nadine cursed.

"Just hold on a second. I may be able to still get in," Chris said.

"How are you going to do that?"

"You're forgetting, I work at the hospital remember? I've seen nurse Johnson get in the system before. She didn't see me watching her put her password and user name in one day while I was working the day shift."Chris got in using the information she so cleverly confiscated from one the unsuspecting nurse.

"Girl, remind me to have you with me if I should ever decide to break into First Eminent Bank's ATM system!" Nadine chuckled.

"Now, who should we look for?" Chris asked.

"Hmm, let's see if we can come up with some information for Rayford that could help out the case. Look for Jade Wilson's files."She typed in Jade's last name and quickly found her files.

"*Jade Salina Wilson, birth date January 23rd 1986 born to Nicolas*

107

and Elva Wilson. Pronounced dead December 12th 2003 10:45 pm. Died from a stab wound to the jugular vein. Blood type B positive," Nadine read out loud. "Oh God,this is too depressing," Nadine moaned.

"You were the one who wanted to do this."

"I know. See if you can find James's records." Chris typed in James's last name. *"James Alexander Duncan, birth date September 3rd. 1985 to James Duncan Sr. and Betty Marie Duncan. Pronounced dead December 13th 2003 11:15 pm. Blood type B positive."*Chris read out loud.

"Wait, I think we may be on to something here. I think I remember reading in the paper that someone else was killed the same night Jade died. I think the paper said her last name was Curtis," Nadine said. She thought for a moment.

"Yeah, that's it. Olivia Curtis. Look for her name."

"Okay."Chris typed in her name. Olivia's file popped up on the computer screen."*Olivia Felicia Curtis, birth date August 6th 1985. Born to Benjamin Curtis and Ethel Leigh Curtis. Pronounced dead December 12th 2003 cause of death strangulation. Blood type, B positive."*

"What is up with the B positive blood type?"asked Nadine.

"I'm calling Rayford," Chris said.

Sharie sat in her car with the engine off in front of Van-Helving's house. She held up her arm and looked at her watch. *Four o'clock. I hope this woman is home. I want to get home in time to do some studying. Mr. Lambert's chemistry class is no joke,* she thought. She checked inside her coat pocket to make sure she had the envelope Rayford gave her, then got out of the car and locked the door and headed to the sidewalk. She paused for a moment to take in her surroundings. *Nice neighborhood*, she thought.

Horsham, Pennsylvania was spacious populated area out side of Philadelphia. A fresh coating of light snow covered the lawns and some of the tree limbs and bushes. Each home along the tree-lined street were newly built. Some homes had aluminum siding on the front and sides, while others were brick laid. Every home had two garages adjoining it either on the left or right side of the house. A few of the houses had several cars sitting in front of the closed garages, others had one. The bay windows or picture windows sat over the garages. Most of the neighbors' homes had two large front doors with two large and round support beams on the left and right. The beams held up the large patios that stood out front. Two other doors lead into the living room from the patio.

Sharie walked up the long walk way to the front door. She rang the doorbell, but no one answered. She was about to ring it again when she noticed the door was ajar. She pushed it open, and walked in cautiously.

"Hello? Is anyone home?" Sharie called into the doorway, she paused and waited for an answer.

"Dr. Van-Helving? Is anybody here?" She walked up a small flight of stairs in front of her, still calling for the doctor. She knew she should just turn around and leave, but she thought whatever was in the envelope was important if Rayford had her come out of school early to bring it to her. At the top of the steps she turned to her right to the living room.

Sharie could tell that Van-Helving was in love with Martha Stewart's products. Everywhere she looked in the living room had Martha Stewart's signature on it. From the pillows that laid on the couch ,down to the arts and crafts things that sat on the tables. She continued through the dining room and through the kitchen. She opened the basement door and saw that the light was on. She called again for the doctor, still no answer. Sharie went downthe steps and looked around then headed for the back of the basement.

The hidden panel was slightly opened Sharie pushed it open and went further down the steps. When she got to the bottom she couldn't figure out why the doctor would leave all of her lights on. She dismissed it and went to the closet door and opened it. *A white doctor's jacket, nothing impressive,* she thought.

Sharie felt around on the top shelf and pulled each item she found out and looked at it, then put them back one by one. *Plastic gloves, rolled bandages, tape, syringes? Why would she have syringes down here and all this other stuff? Wouldn't normal people keep that in a medicine cabinet in there bathrooms?* She thought all of that was odd.

Sharie pushed through other jackets and things that were hanging up and spotted a pair of black shoes. She picked them up and measured them against her own foot. She was about to put them back, when she noticed the dried brownish blood were all over the soles. Sharie remembered seeing in the paper and on the news about the footprints leading from Jade's body the night she was killed. She threw the shoes down and stood up to close the door when Judith appeared from behind the opened door. Sharie screamed and held her chest to try to catch her breath. "Oh, my God, you scared me!"

"Who are you and what are you doing snooping in my closet? Better yet, how did you get in here?"

"My name is Sharie Thompson, ma'am. Your front door was open and I came to drop off this envelope from Detective Rayford," Sharie said. Her voice cracked as she continued to recover from the surprise appearance from Judith.

Sharie stood there bent over in fear, dumb founded for a moment. She didn't realize that the door to the closet was still opened with one shoe sticking out of the door. It was lying on its side with the blood stained sole facing them. Judith looked over Sharie and saw that her secret had been revealed. A sinister smile came on Judith's face as she watched Sharie stand back up to pull out the envelope she had in her back jean's pocket. Sharie had no idea that inside Judith's hospital jacket was a syringe filled with a sedative. Judith waited until Sharie was facing her, then took the syringe and stabbed Sharie in her neck.

"Why did you do that?" Sharie said with fear in her eyes. She felt her neck where the needle entered; the pain surged through her neck and throbbed. Sharie slowly fell to the ground. Judith knelt down to hold her. She put her left arm under Sharie's head, as she lay there under the influence of the drug

"Shhh. I just need one more and then Sarah shall live!"

Sharie looked at the doctor in a total daze. Her face became blurry. Her eyes slowly closed as she slipped into a deep unconsciousness.

CHAPTER 10
PANIC

Rayford drove home from the precinct pondering and thinking about all of the past events of the last few days. He bent over and turned on the radio while he waited at a stoplight. He fumbled around for his favorite jazz station until he found it.

Thoughts about his conversation with Skyler's father, Dr Van-Helving, and Brinkley cluttered his mind. He was happy to have a creep like Brinkley off of the streets. He still couldn't fathom the idea of how he managed to become a teacher, or why Gonzales didn't question him as soon as he found out about the accusations the other kids where spreading around about him. Skyler's father's outburst, during his interview with him, concerned him too. *Was he trying to hide something?* he thought. Then he remembered when he found Brinkley's diary and the news he had heard from Sharie. He played that scene in his apartment over and over again in his head.

"Mr. Rayford, Jade didn't get pregnant by Skyler. She was pregnant by Mr. Brinkley."

"You're kidding me right?"

"No sir. I'm dead serious."

"You know this could be the end of Brinkley's career, right? That's if this is all true, that she was pregnant by him. And that also makes him a prime suspect in this case."

"How?"

"Because for one thing, sweetie, he didn't tell me about the pregnancy and secondly he had sex with a student. But that's not all. I found his diary in his closet with some incriminating evidence as well."

Rayford knew Brinkley was a creep, but a murderer? No, he

couldn't see it. Rayford's gut feeling told him other wise. Rayford turned the corner merging on the expressway towards Center City. He pulled out his cell phone to check on Sharie to make sure she got home all right. He dialed her house number. Her mother picked up the phone.

"Hello?" Mrs. Thompson said.

"Hi, Mrs. Thompson. This is Detective Rayford."

"Oh, hi Detective. What's on your mind?"

"I was wondering if Sharie made it home okay."

"No, she hasn't come home yet and I'm beginning to get a little worried. She never stays out this late without checking in with me and letting me know she's okay."

"Have you tried her cell phone?"

"Yes, but her answering service just picks up."

"I see. When was the last time you talked to her?"

"This afternoon right before she left to take that information over to the doctor. She told me she would be home in time for dinner, but that was an hour ago."

"Don't worry, Mrs. Thompson .I will try to find her and when I do, I'll get back to you. All right?"

"I would appreciate that. Please find her Detective. I won't be able to sleep tonight until I know she's home."

"I will, don't worry." He hung up the phone and jumped over to the next lane for the nearest exit making a U-turn. He headed for Benjamin Bannaker Hospital.

"Chris, don't argue with me," Nadine said while they came off of the elevator and snuck down the hall to the morgue.

"Why didn't she tell Rayford or anybody else about Jade being pregnant? Skyler had the right to know and he shouldn't have found out from Sharie about all of this. Something is not right with this Doctor Van-Helving woman."

"Yeah, but breaking into her office? What are we looking for in there anyway?"

"Files!"

"Oh great! First hacking, now breaking and entering and

ransacking through somebody's personal files! You never cease to amaze me Nadine," Chris said shaking her head. When they found the door to the morgue. It was locked.

"Now what?" Chris asked as she threw her hands up in the air in disgust. Nadine bent down and reached into her right boot she was wearing and pulled out a retractable knife She stood up and looked Chris in the eye.

"I always come prepared! Just watch my back," Nadine said. Chris turned her back to Nadine and kept an eye out for any one coming, while Nadine jimmied the door open. Once they were inside they hurriedly turned on the light and found the file cabinet. That was also locked, but good ol' Nadine pulled out her trusty pocketknife again and popped the file cabinet open. They came across the birth and death certificates of all of the people they had found on the computer up at the nurses' station. Suddenly Chris remembered seeing something on the news a few years ago about Van-Helving.

"Wait. Nadine, see if you can find something under Van-Helving."

"What for?"

"I think you might be on to something, because I remember seeing something about Van-Helving on TV a few years back."

Nadine rifled through the files until she came across the doctor's last name. They found two files and pulled them out, then took them over to the desk with the lamp on it. Nadine paused and took in the room. She could see the stainless steal tables, the refrigerators and the floor coverings that went up the wall. The room was cold and eerie.

"Ew, this place gives me the creeps," Nadine said as she held her arms trying to warm herself.

"Oh, now you're scared! Look, let's just read this thing and get the hell out of here."When they opened the files, they were shocked at what they had found.

"David Van-Helving, Born January 23 1965 Died February 19th 1998. Cause of death, internal injuries due to a car crash," Nadine read out loud. "I knew I saw something about her! Judith Van-Helving was in that car too. But she was the only one who survived.

See what the other file says."

Nadine opened it and they both read out loud."*Sarah Van-Helving Born September 3rd 1984. Died February 22nd 1999. Cause of death, complications due to Acquired Immune Deficiency Syndrome.*" Chris was about to close the file when Nadine spotted something at the bottom of the page, made her gasp.

"What's wrong?" Chris asked.

"Look" Nadine said pointing at the bottom of the page.

"Oh my God! Sarah was B positive! Wait, if I remember correctly the news people said that blood was taken from each victim. Oh, my God! Jade and James were B positive. Could it be possible that we have a psychopathic bitch on our hands?"

"Oh shit! Sharie is over there now! Oh God, Chris help me look around for Van-Helving's address. We've got to get over there!" Nadine closed the files putting them back in the cabinet and then helped Chris go through the drawers to look for Van-Helving's address. They finally came across it and closed the drawer then turned off the light. Both of them raced out the door like grease lighting to help their friend.

~ ~ ~ ~

Sharie lay on the cold floor on her side, unconscious. Her hair plastered to the floor. She began to slowly come out of her deep sleep. Her eyes vaguely open; the room was dark and cold. She tried to get up, but suddenly found her hands tied up behind her back. Van-Helving duct taped her hands and legs. Van-Helving used an old sock of Sarah's and more duct tape to cover Sharie's mouth. *How did I get myself into this shit!* she thought. *I've got to get out of here, but how?* She was still pondering about escaping, when she heard the door open.

The light that came from the door blinded her, but she could see the small woman standing there with a tray in her hand. The smell of meatloaf, peas, and mashed potatoes filled the room. Fear over came Sharie as she tried to back up away from her in a corner of the room. Van-Helving turned on the light to the lab and walked over to the scared and frightened 18-year-old. She bent down in front of her.

"Well, Ms. Thompson. I see you're finally awake," she said as she lay the tray down brushing Sharie's hair back away from her face. Sharie moved her head away from the evil woman.

"I brought you something,"she continued. "I thought you might be a little hungry so I whipped this up for you. Besides, we must get your strength up. We've got a busy night ahead of us and we have to make sure your blood is up to par." Van-Helving reached for Sharie's mouth and ripped the tape off of her lips. Sharie screamed in pain, but the sound went unheard.

"OOPS, I'm sorry did I hurt you angel?"

Sharie pushed the filthy sock out of her mouth. "I know what you did you twisted bitch!"

"Tisk, tisk, tisk, such a trashy mouth for such a beautiful young lady and look at what I brought for you. How unappreciative."

"Fuck off, hoe!"

"Look, why don't we start this all over again? Now, either you can be nice to me and eat your food or I can tie you back up and let you starve to death. Now, what will it be, my sweet?"

Sharie spit in her face. Van-Helving became furious and slapped Sharie. The force of the slap that she gave Sharie sent the young woman flying back into the corner. Sharie's mouth began to bleed, but she couldn't wipe it away.

"Now you listen to me, you little slut! When I come back you'll be sorry for what you just said."

"Oh yeah? Well, you better hope and pray that I never escape! Because if I do, I'll stomp your sick twisted ass into the ground!"

"I don't think so, honey." Van-Helving kicked her tray over to her. "Eat your food."

She stood up and walked back to the door and opened it. She turned back to look at the angered girl lying on the floor.

"When I come back, I'll have a surprise for you!" she said with a sinister smile on her face. Her hideous laughter rang all through the room as she turned out the light and slammed the door. The smell of the food made Sharie's stomach turn. She kicked it away and began to cry.

~ ~ ~ ~

115

Rayford drove down the streets of Philadelphia searching every corner and alley for Sharie's car or hopefully a glimpse of her. He still couldn't shake off the conversation he had with the Doctor.

"When I heard that Ms Wilson was B positive, it made me think of my daughter, Sarah." Then he thought about his conversation with Jake.

"It seems that your killer likes only people with B positive blood." His mind wondered to the phone call he got from Nadine and Chris. *What is it with this B positive blood type?* he thought. Then his mind raced back to the day when he gave Van-Helving the murder weapon and how strangely happy she seemed to have it in her possession. All at once it hit him. *Oh my God! That can't be true! What the hell would Van-Helving want with B positive blood?*

"My daughter Sarah," was the answer he heard in his mind over and over *again. Oh shit! She's crazy if she thinks she can revive her daughter!* But how?...Unless... it all made sense to him now. Rayfor realized the only way she could do it is if Van-Helving had her daughter's body hidden somewhere for all these years. Van-Helving was not at the hospital,and he knew he had to get over to the doctor's home before it was too late.

~ ~ ~ ~

Sharie awoke again, this time in a different room. She noticed that she was lying on something hard and her body was strapped down to it. She could hear the machines running, and she could see the lamp desk light that shone through the glass window in Van-Helvings control room. From the light she could only make out shapes of things that surrounded her, and in a sense she was happy when the doctor entered the room.

Sharie hated being in the dark. Ever since she was a child, her mother kept the night-light on in the hallway of her house, and she always left Sharie's door cracked.

Van-Helving turned on the light and walked over to her victim lying on the stainless steel table.

"Are you ready for your surprise, honey?"

Sharie said nothing. She turned her head away and stared at the two huge tubes that came up from the floor and reached the ceiling beside her.

"Oh, we're quiet all of a sudden. Well, I think I'll put a smile on that cute little face of your's once you see what I have to show you.

"Oh wow! I can't wait to see what you have for me. Mommy can we go bye byes when we're done?" Sharie asked sarcastically.

"DON'T MAKE FUN OF ME! YOU LITTLE BITCH!" Van-Helving's screams shook the room and put the fear of God in Sharie's soul.

"I'M NOT AFRAID OF YOU!" she lied yelling back at her as she looked her in her face.

"You will be when I'm finished with you!"

"Why are you holding me hostage? Huh? What have I ever done to you?"

"Nothing, Sweetie I only need your blood, just like I only needed your friends' blood. Jade was an exceptionally good choice. But I must say it was hard for me to track her down; I mean with school and work and dancing class, whew, Ms. Jade was always on the go, and you know what? I think I could have gotten to her a little bit quicker if your pesky little friend ,Skyler, wasn't always around her. I was sooo happy when he went away with his family. Hell, it helped me get that dumb ass detective off my back for moment. Didn't it?"

Sharie stared at her with nothing but hatred and contempt in her eyes. "You know that 'dumb ass' as you referred to him is going to figure this out, and when he does, he's going to come for me."

"Maybe so, but I'll handle him when he shows up. Now on with the show."

She walked over to the control room and went inside. She turned on the lights and started up the two tubes. The noises scared Sharie even more than she already was. She kicked and pulled to get free, but the straps on her were too tight. Van-Helving turned on the speakers and spoke into her microphone.

"Sit back and enjoy the show, girl. I promise you it'll be better than any horror movie you ever saw! Hell go grab some popcorn while you're at it! Ooops, I forgot you're all tied up there. Oh well."

Nothing could prepare Sharie for the horrifying experience she was about to encounter. She tried not to look, but the lights kept flickering on and off as Van-Helving used all of the electrical juice in her home to bring her daughter up through the tube.

Sharie's eyes widened as the revolting body rose up in front of her. Sarah's eyes were open, which made Sharie turn her face in terror. Sarah's naked body was in full view with tubes running from all over her body. Her hair floated in the liquid solution. Sharie screamed and continued to try to break free to no avail. Van-Helving ran from out of her control room over to where Sharie laid.

"Calm down, you little hussy! Don't you know this is the best thing you could do for another human being?" said Van-Helving.

"What are you going to do with me when you're done?"

"Duh? Kill you, like I did the others you imbecile!"

"Oh, so, you just killed all of my friends for you own selfish reasons? Huh? All because you want your daughter back? Is that it?"

"Yes!"

"Well, it's not going to happen. She's dead! Except it! She's gone Van-Helving and you won't see her again until Judgment Day. That's if you make it!"

"Shut up! I don't want to hear any more of this!"

"WHAT? THE TRUTH? SHE'S DEAD! YOU PSYCHOPATHIC BITCH!"

"I SAID SHUT THE HELL UP!" Van-Helving banged on the metal table with her fist, and then ran hysterically to get the necessary equipment she needed to transfer Sharie's blood.

Sharie tried with all of her might to break free. She didn't notice one side of the strap was cutting on a sharp piece of metal that was slightly sticking out of the side stainless steel gurney she laid upon. She kept pulling and tugging until the one strap broke free.

At first she was amazed at the fact she was free, but then quickly remembered she had only a moment before the psychotic doctor would return. She quickly untied her other arm and legs jumping off the table and ran for the door. She screamed when she opened it and saw Van-Helving standing there with a needle held up in her right hand and a horrible smile on her face.

"Going somewhere?"

She tried to slam the door closed, but the force from Van-Helving kicking it made the door fall off the hinges and knocked Sharie on the floor unconscious. Van-Helving bent down to her fallen victim.

"How dare you try to escape me!" She grabbed Sharie by her hair and dragged her lifeless body across the floor back to the table. She shot her up with a tranquilizer. She got her back up on the table and proceeded to hook her up to the blood-retrieving machine that she created. Dr. Van-Helving laughed horrifically as she inserted the needles and tubes into Sharie's arms. She strapped her down again, this time making sure she couldn't escape her doom.

~ ~ ~ ~

Slowly Sharie began to regain consciousness. She watched in horror as Van-Helving stood in front of the tube, at her beloved Sarah.

"Nothing can stop me now, sweetheart. Soon Mommy will be able to hold you in her arms once again. Oh honey, how I've longed to hold you! This never would have happened if those bratty ass kids hadn't been out joy riding that awful night."

She placed her hands on the glass as if she could feel her daughter's energy. She slowly slid her body down to the floor while still holding her hands on the glass. She sat there for a minute. Her fanatical mind went back to a time when she used to play Jacks on the floor with Sarah. She could see her daughter sitting in front of her in her demented mind. She gestured throwing the ball up while her other hand grabbed for the jack on the floor.

"Mommy's not going to let you beat me again," she said out loud in a sly voice. She laughed as she envisioned her child trying to do everything she could to win. Her smile quickly turned into a glare when she looked up and saw her victim half awake. She crawled over to Sharie as if she were a cheetah about to pounce on her prey. She pulled herself up on the table slowly and stared at Sharie.

"Soon Daddy will be home, honey. And Mommy has to go and welcome him, but first we have to take care of one itty bitty problem."

"Please don't hurt me! Please let me go!" Sharie said crying and pleading.

"I'm afraid I can't do that, sweetie, but this won't hurt a bit you'll see." Van-Helving walked away from her back toward the control room.

"Please let me go!" Sharie screamed as she watched her walk away. But her pleads of mercy fell on deaf ears. All Sharie could do now was pray for her rescuers to come...

CHAPTER 11
DEATH BECOMES HER

Nadine and Chris ran up to the doctors' front door. They banged on it demanding entrance. "Van-Helving open this damn door! We know you're in there!" Nadine yelled. Silence came from the other side of the door while they continued banging. "You've got ten seconds before we kick this mother fucker down!" Chris yelled.

All of a sudden the door mysteriously opened. Nadine ran in first with Chris at her heels. "Where the hell are you? You sick witch!" The sound of an eerie laughter rang out around them.

The room was shadowy, only the light shining from the street lamps outside through a window could be seen through the living room. Chris examined the room.

"Damn, it looks like somebody's in love with K-Mart!"

"Chris, will you come on! We have to find Sharie. God only knows what the hell she's done with her." They slowly treaded through the rooms until they found the door to the basement. Nadine opened the door.

"Shit, where's the light?"

"I don't know.r I bought my key chain with my light on it."

"Could you please turn it on?" Chris said sarcastically.

Nadine dug in her pocket until she found her keys and then turned on the little flashlight. They could barely see what was in front of them.

"That doesn't help much!" Chris said.

"Look, that's all we've got ok! Now shut up and help look for Sharie." Chris wanted to slap her in the back of head, but decided to wait until another time. They slowly descended down the steps entering the room with the secret wall. They went in holding each other close. They were amazed at there findings.

"What the hell is all this crap? What are all these machines and look over there; those two tubes are humongous!" Nadine cried out.

"I don't know, looks like some kind of..."The girls' attention focused on the life less form of their friend lying on the table.

"Sharie!" Nadine yelled. They ran over to her and unloosed the straps that were holding her down. Chris scooped her arm under Sharie's head and held her tightly. Nadine laid her keys down next to her. They tried to undo all of the tubes that came out from her when Van-Helving flew out of the control room.

"Not so fast, young ladies."

":I was hoping you two would show up!"

"What have you done to her?"Chris yelled.

"The same thing I'll do to you or anybody else who stands in my way!"

Anger blinded Nadine and she ran up to Van-Helving with intentions to kill. "You evil bitch!" She swung at her with her fist, but Van-Helving ducked and counter suited with a left into Nadine's face, sending her flying across the floor.

Chris laid Sharie down to go after Van-Helving but, before she could lay a finger on her, Chris found herself staring down the barrel of a Saturday night special.

"Don't move or I'll blow your fuckin head off! Now have a seat and watch the show!"

Chris sat on the floor by the wall in front of the control room. Nadine sat up on the floor holding her head in pain. She slid over to Chris

"I swear if I get out of this alive, your ass is mine!" Nadine yelled.

"You know, you sure do have a lot of guts for somebody who has a gun pointed to her head. I like that in a girl, here let me wipe that off your mouth," Van-Helving said reaching down to trying to touch her, still keeping the gun on Chris.

Nadine remembered she still had her pocketknife in her boot. She waited until Van-Helving was close enough, then pulled it out and attempted to stab her in the stomach. Van-Helving saw it coming and grabbed Nadine's arm.

"You sneaky little slut!"She pistol-whipped Nadine. Then got up and signaled for Chris to get in front of her and head to the control room. "Now you will see the wonders of modern technology," Van-Helving said keeping the gun trained on Chris while flipping the switch to let the blood transfusion begin. The blood began to flow slowly from Sharie down through the tubes on the floor and up to the hydraulic chamber and into Sarah.

"You stupid bitch! She won't come back to life! I don't care how much blood you give her. She's been dead too long!" Chris said as she stood in the corner in the shadow of the room.

"Oh, but you don't know about my other little secret."

"What the hell are you talking about?"

"Shut up and get over here next to me!"

Chris did as she was told. Van-Helving went over to the closet and pulled out her black robe with one button missing. Reaching over the shelf and grabbed her black magic book of spells. She brought it over to the control panel and opened it up to the page she needed and memorized it. She laid the gun on the panel and looked up at the ceiling with her hands stretched up and out. She began speaking in an unknown language that Chris knew nothing about.

"Ahsyek ardnasirhc aicilef allemaj aicirtap!"

The room started to shake from the evil that engulfed it. The lights flickered on and off while Van-Helving continued to chant screaming to the top of her lungs. Her body started to shake from the evil that was being transferred into her soul.

Fear struck Chris's body as she turned to look out of the window. The chamber that held Sarah had begun to bubble frantically. Sharie lay on the table slowly coming out of her deep sleep. She could vaguely make out what was going on. She looked over at the tubes filled with her blood watching it slowly leave her body. She screamed and recklessly tried to break free. Nadine awoke and tried to run to her friend, but the vibrations from the evil spirit that consumed the room caused her to slip and fall and hit her head on the table, causing her to black out before she could reach her.

The chamber that held Sarah shattered, her body broke free and fell on the floor. She started to breathe. She was alive! Van-Helving looked out of the window at her child lying on the floor. She ran out of the room to help her. But Chris's fear turned into anger. She tripped her as she tried to get out of the door and then landed a right hook square to her jaw. Van-Helving fell back un-phased and retaliated punching Chris in her stomach, which made her double over and fall back and hit the wall. She was out momentarily. Van-Helving continued out of the door towards her child. She bent down to pick her up as blood ran profusely around the floor. Fluid from the chamber bursted causing the machines to spark and catch on fire. Van-Helving held her daughter in her arms and looked her in the eye. She could see she was breathing on her own.

"Sarah! You're alive! Oh my precious baby!"

"Mommy?" she said.

"Yes, honey it's me."She wiped the water from her face and nose and brushed her hair back with her hands and hugged her. Van-Helving was so over come with joy that she didn't see Rayford come into the room with his 22-Magnum drawn.

Rayford saw Sharie on the table and Nadine beside it. He rushed over to help them. Rayford was untying Sharie ,when he looked over the table at Van-Helving. "What the hell's going on here?" said Rayford

"Oh it's such a wonderful thing! Don't you think?" she smiled up at him as she sat there holding her daughter. "My daughter's alive, Rayford! She's alive!" she said laughing.

"What have you done to these girls?" he said pointing his gun at her.

"Only what they deserved."

He finished untying Sharie and went on the other side to help Nadine. He bent down and held her then shook her until she awoke. She told Rayford what had happened. He became furious, "You crazy sun of a…!"

Van-Helving was gone.

Nadine looked up at the wall and noticed a sword inside of a glass case. She turned back and looked at Rayford. "Go and find that crazy woman. I'll be fine."

"Are you sure?"

"Yes I'm sure. Go!"

Rayford picked up his gun next to him and got up. He saw Van-Helving in the control room and ran in. But this time Van-Helving was ready for him. She was on the floor with Chris. Her gun pointed directly at him. She held Chris, who was crying in between her legs. They both sat facing him. Van-Helving held a needle in her other hand, her arm was wrapped around Chris's neck with the needle almost touching Chris's neck. "This needle is filled with poison Rayford! Make one move and I swear to God I'll stick her! Now drop your gun and kick it over to me."

He dropped it and kicked it to her. Van-Helving pushed herself and Chris up using the wall for support. "Now, open the door and put your hands up where I can see them and go back out."

Rayford stood there for a moment.

"Do it I said! Or she's dead!" she clutched Chris's neck even tighter. Chris wanted to scream, but couldn't.

They came back out into the lab. Rayford saw that Sharie was still lying on the table. She couldn't move. She needed blood badly. Only a blood transfusion would save her.

Where is my back up and the ambulance? Rayford thought. *I called them 20 minutes ago. Damn! If you want shit done right, you have to do it yourself!* He looked around the room and noticed that Nadine was gone. He remembered seeing her look up at the wall and noticed that the sword was gone also. *Where the hell is she?*

Van-Helving also noticed that Nadine was gone, but didn't say anything or think anything of it.

I will get her in due time, she thought. Van-Helving let Chris go and pushed her towards Rayford.

"Now both of you get up against the wall!" She slowly backed up towards the desk that was in the room, then bent down to opened the drawer. She fished around for the duct tape and found it. She made sure their backs where turned, and pulled off two long strips. She walked back up to them and had them put their hands behind their backs, then she taped their hands together. First Rayford then Chris.

"Turn around and have a seat," she said. "I have more work to do, and I don't want to hear shit from either of you! Is that understood?"

"You know, I used to think you were a beautiful woman, Van-Helving. But now my mother in-law makes you look like dog crap!"

"Well, Mr. Rayford, thank you for the compliment… I think, oh and when you get to hell, which by the way is where I'm going to send you, tell you're mother in-law, which I'm sure she'll be there with you, that at least my dog shit looks better then your simple ass!" she said with a scowl on her face. She got up and looked around the room. "Now where is that little Ms. Nadine?" Judith went around the room searching for her. "Come out, come out where ever you are!"

Nadine laid low behind the once two chambers, except she was behind the one that wasn't broken. The huge computer machine helped keep her hidden, so hidden that Van-Helving didn't see her crouched down with the sword behind her until it was too late. As soon as Van-Helving turned and saw Nadine she fired her gun, but miraculously missed her target. She kept shooting, but to her demise the gun had gone empty. Nadine pulled the sword from behind her and jumped up and lunged forward toward Van-Helving. Nadine aimed for her neck.

"This is for Jade you evil manipulative BITCH!"she cried. With one quick swipe she sent her head over the machine and over Sharie. It landed on the floor. Nadine ran to untie Rayford and Chris. In turn they untied Sharie. No one expected the horrible scene of the decapitated body of Van-Helving still standing up walking unsteadily towards them. Rayford shot at it until his gun was empty. He stood there still firing the empty gun, when Chris reached over and grabbed his arm.

"It's over Rayford! She's dead."

He slowly put the gun down and walked over to Sharie. "An ambulance should be here any moment."

They were all hovering over Sharie when the ambulance and

police back up finally came. The paramedics took her away to the nearest hospital, where she was listed in stable condition. Rayford, Chris, and Nadine stayed behind to go through the formalities of explaining what had happened to them to the men in blue. Rayford took a moment from the crime scene to call Sharie's mother and informed her as to what happened and where her daughter would be. Captain Jennings came in and congratulated Rayford and all of the girls for their outstanding bravery.

"Rayford, you've got some explaining to do!"

"What do you mean, Sir?"

"How did these young ladies get in here? Don't you realize they could have been killed?"

Rayford grabbed Nadine who was standing next to him and Chris who stood on the other side and hugged them tightly.

"Who? Theses girls?"

Chris and Nadine looked at Rayford and smiled. They all shook their heads and said in unison. "NAH!"

EPILOGUE

Ten years later...

Sarah Van-Helving sat at the control panel in her mother's lab looking over the book of spells the doctor had left behind. She found it while cleaning out the desk drawers in the lab. She had spent several years in the psychiatric ward of a prestigious hospital in Newark, New Jersey. The doctors felt that she was competent enough to go and start a new life; a new life in a new city, but Sarah had other plans that she didn't inform the doctors or anybody else of.

She got up and went out to the lab area. She managed to fix the broken tube that once incased her dead body. She looked up at it and smiled wickedly at it. The table that once held Sharie now had another figure on it; it was covered in a white sheet. She laughed at how cleverly she had stolen the body out of the grave. Sarah walked up to the dead corpse lying there and lifted the sheet back down to the shoulders. The mortician now sewed its previously decapitated head on to its body. The face was blue and decaying, maggots crawled out of one its eye and out of its mouth. Flies swarmed around the entire head. Sarah bent down and looked into her mother's eyes. She stroked back the dead red hair that lay across her forehead. She began to recite the spell that brought her back years before.

"Ahsyek ardnasirhc aicilef allemaj aicirtap!"

She said it over and over again, each time louder than before. The lights in the room started to flicker as the evil had once again engulfed the room.

She looked down at her mother and observed, as she watched her mother's eyes appear and then within a flash they were open! Sarah gasped and dropped the book of spells as she watched her mother sit up and reach for her and laugh hysterically.

"Come to me my child!"

Sarah hesitated then slowly reached out for her and hugged her.

"Now, my child we must avenge my killers!"

"Yes momma, indeed we shall!"

They hugged each other tightly and laughed violently at the evil fun they were about to explore.

Printed in the United Kingdom
· Lightning Source UK Ltd.
37UKS00001B/11